AIR SERVICE BOYS OVER THE RHINE

BY

CHARLES AMORY BEACH

AIR SERVICE BOYS OVER THE RHINE

CHAPTER I

DOUBLE NEWS

"Here they come back, Tom!"

"Yes, I see them coming. Can you count them yet? Don't tell me any of our boys are missing!" and the speaker, one of two young men, wearing the uniform of the Lafayette Escadrille, who were standing near the hangars of the aviation field "somewhere in France," gazed earnestly up toward the blue sky that was dotted with fleecy, white clouds.

There were other dots also, dots which meant much to the trained eyes of Tom Raymond and Jack Parmly, for the dots increased in size, like oncoming birds. But they were not birds. Or rather, they were human birds.

The specks in the sky were Caudrons. A small aerial fleet was returning from a night raid over the German ammunition dumps and troop centers, and the anxiety of the watching young men was as to whether or not all the airmen, among whom were numbered some of Uncle Sam's boys, had returned in safety. Too many times they did not—that is not all—for the Hun anti-aircraft guns found their marks with deadly precision at times.

The Caudrons appeared larger as they neared the landing field, and Tom and Jack, raising their binoculars, scanned the ranks—for all the world like a flock of wild geese—to see if they could determine who of their friends, if any, were missing.

"How do you make it, Tom?" asked Jack, after an anxious pause.

"I'm not sure, but I can count only eight."

"That's what I make it. And ten of 'em went out last night, didn't they?"

"So I heard. And if only eight come back it means that at least four of our airmen have either been killed or captured."

"One fate is almost as bad as the other, where you have to be captured by the Boches," murmured Jack. "They're just what their name indicates— beasts!"

"You said something!" came heartily from Tom. "And yet, to the credit of airmen in general, let it be said that the German aviators treat their fellow, prisoners better than the Hun infantrymen do."

"So I've heard. Well, here's hoping neither of us, nor any more of our friends, falls over the German lines. But look, Tom!" and Jack pointed excitedly. "Are my eyes seeing things, or is that another Caudron looming up there, the last in the line? Take a look and tell me. I don't want to hope too much, yet maybe we have lost only one, and not two."

Tom changed the focus of his powerful glasses slightly and peered in the direction indicated by his chum. Then he remarked, with the binoculars still at his eyes:

"Yes, that's another of our machines! But she's coming in slowly. Must have been hit a couple of times."

"She's lucky, then, to get back at all. But let's go over and hear what the news is. I hope they blew up a lot of the Huns last night."

"Same here!"

The aircraft were near enough now for the throbbing of their big motors to be heard, and Tom and Jack, each an officer now because of gallant work, hurried across the landing field.

It was early morning, and they had come, after a night's rest, to report for duty with others of the brave Americans who, during the neutrality of this country in the great conflict, went to France as individuals, some to serve as ambulance drivers, others to become aviators.

The Caudron is the name given to one type of heavy French aeroplane carrying two or more persons and tons of explosive bombs.

An air raid on the German lines by a fleet of these machines had been planned. It had been timed for an early hour of the night, but a mist coming up just as the squadron of heavy machines, each with two men and a ton or more of explosives, was ready to set out, the hour had been changed. So it was not until after midnight that the start had been made.

And now the boys were coming back—that is all who were able to return. One machine was missing. At least, that was the assumption of Tom and Jack, for they could count but nine where there should have been ten. And of the nine one was coming back so slowly as to indicate trouble.

One by one the machines, which ordinarily came back before daybreak, landed, and the pilot and the observer of each climbed clumsily down from their cramped seats. They were stiff with cold, in spite of the fur-lined garments they wore—garments that turned them, for the moment, into animated Teddy bears, or the likeness of Eskimos.

Their faces were worn and haggard, for the strain of an airship bombing raid is terrific. But they were quiet and self-possessed as they walked stiffly across the field to make a report.

"Any luck?" asked Tom, of one he knew; a Frenchman noted for his skill and daring.

"The best, mon ami," he replied with a smile—a weary smile. "We gave Fritz a dose of bitter medicine last night."

"And he gave us a little in return," sadly added his companion. "Quarre and Blas—" he shrugged his shoulders, and Tom and Jack knew what it meant.

They were the men in the missing machine, the Caudron that had not come back.

"Did you see what happened?" asked Jack.

Picard, to whom Tom had first spoken, answered briefly.

"They caught them full in the glare of a searchlight and let them have it. We saw them fall. There didn't seem to be any hope."

"But the battery that did the firing—it is no more," added De Porry, the companion of Picard. "The bombs that Quarre and Blas carried went down like lead, right on top of the Hun guns. They are no more, those guns and those who served."

"It was a retributive vengeance," murmured Picard.

Then they passed on, and others, landing, also went to make their reports.

Some of them had reached their objectives, and had dropped the bombs on the German positions in spite of the withering fire poured upward at them. Others had failed. There is always a certain percentage of failures in a night bombing raid. And some were unable to say with certainty what damage they had caused.

The last slowly flying machine came to a landing finally, and there was a rush on the part of the other aviators to see what had happened. When Tom and Jack saw a limp form being lifted out, and heard murmurs of admiration for the pilot who had brought his machine back with a crippled engine, they realized what had happened.

The two brave men had fulfilled their mission; they had released their bombs over an important German factory, and had the terrible satisfaction of seeing it go up in flames. But on their return they had been caught in a cross fire, and the observer, who was making his first trip of this kind, had been instantly killed.

The engine had been damaged, and the pilot slightly wounded, but he had stuck to his controls and had brought the machine back.

There was a little cheer for him, and a silent prayer for his brave companion, and then the night men, having made their reports, and having divested themselves of their fur garments, went to rest.

"Well, what's on the programme for to-day, Tom?" asked Jack, as they turned back toward the hangars where they had their headquarters with others of their companions in the Lafayette Escadrille and with some of the French birdmen.

"I don't know what they have on for us. We'll have to wait until the orders come in. I was wondering if we would have time to go and see if there's any mail for us."

"I think so. Let's go ask the captain."

They had, of course, reported officially when they came on duty, and now they went again to their commanding officer, to ask if they might go a short distance to the rear, where an improvised post-office had been set up for the flying men.

"Certainly, messieurs," replied the French captain, when Tom proffered the request for himself and his chum. "Go, by all means." He spoke in French, a good mastery of which had been acquired by our heroes since their advent into the great war. "Your orders have not yet arrived, but hold yourselves in readiness. Fritz is doubtless smarting under the dose we gave him last night, and he may retaliate. There is a rumor that we may go after some of his sausages, and I may need you for that."

"Does he mean our rations have gone short, and that we'll have to go collecting bolognas?" innocently asked a young American, who had lately joined.

"No," laughed Tom. "We call the German observation balloons 'sausages.' And sometimes, when they send up too many of them, to get observations and spoil our plans for an offensive, we raid them. It's difficult work, for we have to take them unawares or they'll haul them down. We generally go in a double squadron for this work. The heavy Caudrons screen the movements of the little Nieuports, and these latter, each with a single man in it, fire phosphorus bullets at the gas bags of the German sausages.

"These phosphorus bullets get red hot from the friction of the air, and set the gas envelope aglow. That starts the hydrogen gas to going and—good-night to Mr. Fritz unless he can drop in his parachute. A raid on the sausages is full of excitement, but it means a lot of preparation, for if there has any rain or dew fallen in the night the gas bags will be so damp that they can't be set on fire, and the raid is off."

"Say, you know a lot about this business, don't you?" asked the young fellow who had put the question.

"Nobody knows a lot about it," replied Jack. "Just as soon as he does he gets killed, or something happens to him. We're just learning—that's all."

"Well, I wish I knew as much," observed the other enviously.

Tom and Jack walked on toward the post-office, being in rather a hurry to see if there was any mail for them, and to get back to their stations in case their services were needed.

As they went along they were greeted by friends, of whom they had many, for they had made names for themselves, young as they were. And, as a matter of fact, nearly all the aviators are young. It takes young nerves for the work.

"Here's one letter, anyhow!" observed Tom, as he tore open a missive that was handed to him. "It's from dad, too! I hope he's all right. He must have been when he wrote this, for it's in his own hand."

"I've got one from my mother," said Jack. "They're all well," he went on, quickly scanning the epistle. "But they haven't received our last letters."

"That isn't surprising," said Tom. "The mail service is fierce. But I suppose it can't be helped. We're lucky to get these. And say!" he exclaimed excitedly, as he read on in his letter. "Here's news all right—great news!"

Jack looked at his chum. Tom's face was flushed. The news seemed to be pleasurable.

Jack was about to ask what it was, when he saw a messenger running from the telephone office. This was the main office, or, at least, one of the main offices, in that section, and official, as well as general, news was sometimes sent over the wire.

The man was waving a slip of paper over his head, and he was calling out something in French.

"What's he saying?" asked Jack.

"Something about good news," answered Tom. "I didn't get it all. Let's go over and find out. It's good news all right," he went on. "See! they're cheering."

"More news," murmured Jack. "And you have some, too?"

"I should say so! Things surely are happening this morning! Come on!" and Tom set off on a run.

CHAPTER II

ANXIOUS DAYS

While Tom and Jack were hastening toward the man who seemed to have received some message, telephone, telegraph or wireless, from the headquarters of this particular aviation section, a throng of the aviators, their mechanicians, and various helpers, had surrounded the messenger and were eagerly listening to what he had to say.

"I wonder what it can be, Tom," murmured Jack, as the two fairly ran over the field.

Those of you who have read the two preceding volumes of this series will remember Tom Raymond and Jack Parmly. As related in the first book, "Air Service Boys Flying for France; or The Young Heroes of the Lafayette Escadrille," the youths had, some time previously, gone to a United States aviation school in Virginia, their native state, and there had learned the rudiments of managing various craft of the air. Tom's father was an inventor of note, and had perfected a stabilizer for an aeroplane that was considered very valuable, so much so that a German spy stole one of the documents relating to the patent.

It was Tom's effort to get possession of this paper that led him and, incidentally, his chum Jack into many adventures. From their homes in Bridgeton, Virginia, they eventually reached France and were admitted into that world-famed company—the Lafayette Escadrille. Putting themselves under the tuition of the skilled French pilots, the Air Service boys forged rapidly to the front in their careers.

It was while on a flight one day that they attacked a man in a motor car, who seemed to be acting suspiciously along the sector to which our heroes were assigned, and they pursued him, believing him to be a German spy.

Their surmise proved correct, for the man, who was hurt when his machine got beyond control, was none other than Adolph Tuessig, the German who had vainly tried to buy Mr. Raymond's stabilizer from him, and who had, later, stolen the paper.

In our second volume, entitled, "Air Service Boys Over the Enemy's Lines; or The German Spy's Secret," Tom and Jack found further adventures. On their way to England, whence they had gone to France, they had met on the steamer a girl named Bessie Gleason. She was in the company of Carl Potzfeldt. The girl seemed much afraid of him, though he was her guardian, said to have been so named by Mrs. Gleason, a distant relative of his. Mrs. Gleason had been on the ill-fated Lusitania, and it was related by Potzfeldt, for purposes of his own, that Bessie's mother had been drowned. Moreover, he declared that before she died she had given him charge of Bessie.

Tom and Jack, the latter especially, grew very fond of Bessie, but there seemed to be a mystery about her and something strange in her fear of her guardian.

When the two young men reached England, they lost sight, for a time, of their fellow passengers, but they were destined to meet them again under strange circumstances.

During one of their flights they landed near a lonely house behind the German lines. They were traveling in a Caudron, which contained them both, and on investigating the building after dark they found, to their surprise, that Bessie and her mother were kept there, prisoners of Carl Potzfeldt, who was a German spy.

Bessie and her mother were rescued and then departed for Paris, the latter to engage in Red Cross work, and the boys, remaining with their fellow aviators, longed for the time when they might see their friends once more.

But they had enlisted to help make the world safe for democracy, and they intended to stay until the task was finished. Over a year had elapsed since the sensational rescue of Bessie and her mother. The United States had entered the war and the Air Service boys were thinking that soon they might be able to join an American aviation service in France.

"What is it? What has happened?" Tom demanded of one of the aviators on the outskirts of the throng about the messenger. "Have we won a victory over the Germans?"

"No, but we're going to," was the answer. "Oh, boy! It's great! We're in it now sure! Hurray!"

"In it? What do you mean?" asked Jack.

"I mean that Uncle Sam has at last stepped over the line! He's sure enough on the side of the Allies now, and no mistake."

"You mean—" cried Tom.

"I mean," answered Ralph Nelson, another American aviator, "that the United States has made a big success of the Liberty Bonds loan and is going to send a million soldiers over here as soon as possible! Say, isn't that great?"

"Great? I should say so!" fairly yelled Tom. "Shake!" he cried, and he and his chum and everybody else shook hands with every one whose palm they could reach. And there were resounding claps on the back, and wild dances around the green grass, even the French joining in. No not that word "even," for the French, with their exuberance of spirit, really started the joy-making.

To the brave men, who, with the British, had so long endured the brunt of the terrible blows of the Huns alone, the efforts of the United States of America meant much, though it was realized that it would be some time before Uncle Sam could make his blows really tell, even though an Expeditionary Force was already in the field.

"Say, this is the best news ever!" said Jack to Tom, when quiet, in a measure, had been restored. "It's immense!"

"You said something, old man! It's almost as good news as if you had come in and told me that you had downed a whole squadron of German aircraft."

"I wish I could, Tom. But we'll do our share. Shouldn't wonder, before the day is out, but what we'd get orders to go up and see what we can spot. But I'm almost forgetting. You had some news of your own."

"Yes, I have. And now I have a chance to finish reading dad's letter."

"But first you can tell me what the special news is, can't you?" asked Jack. "That is, unless you think it will be too much for me to stand all in one day—your news and that about Uncle Sam's success in raising funds and troops."

"Oh, I guess you can stand it," said Tom with a smile. "It's this. Dad is coming over!"

"He is? To fight?"

"Well, no, not actively. He's a little too old for that, I'm afraid, though he's anxious enough. But he left for Paris the day he wrote this. He ought to be here now, for he would, most likely, get off ahead of the mail, which, sometimes, seems slower than molasses."

"That's right!" exclaimed Jack, with such energy that Tom asked:

"What's the matter? Haven't you heard from Bessie lately?"

"Oh—that!" murmured Jack, but Tom noticed that his friend blushed under his coat of tan. "Go on," Jack said, a moment later, "tell me about your father. Is the French government going to give him a big order for his stabilizer, now that we got that paper away from that sneak of a Tuessig?"

"Well, I guess dad's trip here has something to do with his aeroplane device, but he hints in his letter about something else. He said he didn't want to write too much for fear a spy might get hold of the information. But you know my father is an expert on ordnance matters and big guns, as well as in other lines of fighting."

"That's so, Tom. He certainly is a wonder when it comes to inventing things. But what do you suppose his new mission is?"

"I can't quite guess. But it is for the service of the Allies."

"And you say he's on his way to Paris now?"

"He ought to be there by this time," Tom answered. "I'm going to see if I can't get permission to send a message through, and have an answer from dad. Maybe he might get out here to see us."

"Or we could go in and meet him."

"Not for a week. You know we just came back from leave, and we won't be over our tour of duty for seven days more. But I can't wait that long without some word. I'm going to see what I can find out."

Tom and Jack, like all the other American fliers, were in high favor with the French officers. In fact every aviator of the Allied nations, no matter how humble his rank, is treated by his superiors almost as an equal. There is not that line of demarcation noticed in other branches of the service. To be an aviator places one, especially in England and France, in a special class. All regard him as a hero who is taking terrible risks for the safety of the other fighters.

So Tom readily received permission to send a message to the hotel in Paris mentioned by his father as the place where Mr. Raymond would stay. And then Tom had nothing to do but wait for an answer.

Nothing to do? No, there was plenty. Both Tom and Jack had to hold themselves in readiness for instant service. They might be sent out on a bombing expedition at night in the big heavy machines, slow of flight but comparatively safe from attack by other aircraft.

They might have the coveted honor of being selected to go out in the swift, single Nieuports to engage in combat with some Hun flier. To become an "ace"—that is a birdman who, flying alone, has disposed of five enemies—is the highest desire of an aviator.

Tom and Jack, eager and ambitious, were hoping for this.

Again, in the course of the day's work, they might be selected to go up in the big bi-motored Caudrons for reconnoissance work. This is dangerous and hard. The machines carry a wireless apparatus, over which word is sent back to headquarters concerning what may be observed of the enemy's defenses, or a possible offensive.

Often the machines go beyond the range of their necessarily limited wireless, and have to send back messages by carrier pigeons which are carried on the craft.

By far the most dangerous work, however, is that of "relage" or fire control. This means that two men go up in a big machine that carries a large equipment. Their craft is heavy and unwieldy, and has such a spread of wing surface that it is not easily turned, and if attacked by a German Fokker has little chance of escape. A machine gun is carried for defense.

It is a function of those in the machine to send word back to the battery officers of the effect of the shots they are firing, that the elevation and range may be corrected. And those who go out on "relage" work are in danger not only from the fire of the enemy's batteries, but often, also, from their own.

Tom and Jack had their share of danger and glory during the week they were on duty following the receipt of the two pieces of news. They went up together and alone, and once, coming back from a successful trip over the enemy's lines, Tom's machine was struck by several missiles. His cheek was cut by one, and his metal stability control was severed so that his craft started to plunge.

Tom thought it was his end, but he grasped the broken parts of the control rod in one hand, and steered with the other, bringing his machine down behind his own lines, amid the cheers of his comrades.

"And I'm glad to be back, not only for my sake, but for the sake of the machine. She's a beauty, and I'd have hated like anything to set fire to her," remarked Tom, after his wound had been dressed.

He referred to the universal practice of all aviators of setting fire to their craft if they are brought down within the enemy lines, and are not so badly injured as to prevent them from opening the gasoline tank and setting a match to it. This is done to prevent the machine, and often the valuable papers or photographs carried, from falling into the hands of the enemy.

The end of the week came, the last of seven anxious days, and it was time for Tom and Jack to be relieved for a rest period. And the days had been anxious because Tom had not heard from his father.

"I hope the vessel he was coming on wasn't torpedoed," said Tom to his chum. "He's had more than time to get here and send me some word. None has come. Jack, I'm worried!" And Tom certainly looked it.

CHAPTER III

ON TO PARIS

Those were the days—and they had been preceded by many such—when travel across the Atlantic was attended with great risk and uncertainty. No one knew when a lurking German submarine might loose a torpedo at a ship carrying men, women and children. Many brave and innocent people had found watery graves, and perhaps suffered first a ruthless fire from the German machine guns, which were even turned on lifeboats! So it was no wonder that Tom Raymond was worried about his father.

"It's queer we can't get any word from the authorities in Paris," remarked Jack, as he and his chum were speculating one day on what might have happened.

"Yes, and that helps to bother me," Tom admitted. "It isn't as if they weren't trying, for the officers here have done all they can. They've gotten off my messages, but they say there is no reply to them."

"Then it must mean that your father, if he is in Paris, hasn't received them."

"Either that, Jack; or else he doesn't dare reply."

"Why wouldn't he dare to, Tom?"

"Well, I don't know that I can give a good reason. It might be that he is on such a secret mission that he doesn't want even to hint about it. And yet I can't understand why he doesn't send me at least a message that he has arrived safely."

As Tom said this he looked at his chum. The same thought was in the mind of each one:

Had Mr. Raymond arrived safely?

That was what stirred Tom's heart. He knew the danger he and Jack had run, coming across to do their part in flying for France, and he well realized that the Germans might have been more successful in attacking the vessel on which his father had sailed, than they had the one which had carried Tom and Jack.

"Well, what are we going to do?" asked Jack of his chum. "You know we arranged, when we should get our leave, to go back to that pretty little French village, which seemed so peaceful after all the noise of battle and the roar of the aeroplane engines."

"Yes, I know we planned that," said Tom, reflectively. "But, somehow, I feel that I ought to stay here."

"And not take our relief?"

"Oh, no. We'll take that," decided Tom. "We must, in justice to ourselves, and those we work with. You know they tell us an airman must always be at his best, with muscles and nerves all working together. And a certain amount of rest and change are necessary, after a week or so of steady flying. So we'll take our rest in order to be in all the better shape to trim the Fritzies. But I was thinking of staying right here."

"And not go back into the country?" asked Jack.

Tom shook his head.

"I'd like to stay right here until I get word from my father," he said. "He may send a message at any time, and he knows I am stationed here. Of course I could send him word that we're having a little vacation, and give him our new address.

"But the mails are so mixed up, and the telegraph and telephone systems are so rushed, that he might not get it. So I think the best thing will be to stay right here where I'll be on hand to get it the moment word comes. But don't let me keep you, Jack. You can go, if you want to."

"Say, what do you think I am?" cried his chum. "Where you stick, I stick! We'll both wait here for word from your father. I have a sort of feeling that he is all right."

"Well, to tell you the truth, I suppose he is. But, at the same time, I'm worried. I can't explain it, but I have a sort of sense that he is in danger."

"Not if he is in Paris, Tom. The German's haven't gotten within striking distance of that city yet, in spite of their boasts—the boasts of the Kaiser and of the Crown Prince."

"No, if dad were in Paris I'd feel that he was comparatively safe. But first I want to know that he is. And yet, even if he has put up at that house in the Rue Lafayette, where he said in his letter he'd stay, there may be some danger."

"Danger in Paris? What do you mean, Tom?"

"Well, Paris has been bombed from the air, you know."

"True, Tom. But, say! we've almost come to disregard such mild things as that from the Huns, haven't we?"

"Well, we'll just stay right on here," decided Tom. "I don't mean to say that we'll stay around our hangar all the while, but we'll keep in touch, throughout the day, with the communication headquarters. Dad may send a message at any time, and I want to get it as soon as it arrives."

Jack could understand his chum's feelings, and so the Air Service boys, who, some time previous, had sought and received permission to go back several kilometers into the country for a rest, announced that they would stay on at the aerodrome.

Nor did they lack excitement. The place where they were stationed was a busy one. For every twenty pilots and observers there are detailed about one hundred men as helpers. There are cooks, photographers, mechanics of various sorts, telephone, telegraph and wireless operators, orderlies and servants.

Of these Tom and Jack had their share, for it is the business of an airman to fly and fight, and he does nothing except in that line. He is catered to and helped in every possible way when not in the air. He has some one to wait on him, to look after his machine, and to attend to his hurts, if he is unlucky enough to get any. Of course each flier goes over, personally, his own craft, but he has oilers and mechanics to do all the detail work.

"Well, there they go!" exclaimed Tom to Jack one morning, the second of their "vacation," as they observed a number of "aces" about to go up and search above the clouds for some Hun to attack.

"Yes, and I wish I was with them!" said Jack.

"Waiting isn't much fun," agreed his chum. "I'm sure I can't understand why dad doesn't send some word. If this keeps up much longer—Say, Jack, look at Parla!" he suddenly cried. "What's the matter with him?"

Jack looked. The men, in their machines, had started off to get momentum for a rise into the air. But there had been a rain and the ground was soft, which kept down the speed. All the pilots seemed to get off in fairly good shape except one, Parla by name, who had only recently secured the coveted designation of "ace."

And then occurred one of those tragedies of flying. Whether he was nervous at taking a flight in such distinguished company, or whether something went wrong with Parla's machine never would be known.

He was the last in the line, and as it was rather misty he might have been anxious not to lose sight of his companions. He did not take a long enough run, and when he reached the end of the field he was not high enough to clear the line of hangars that were in front of him.

Some one shouted at him, not stopping to realize that the noise of the motor drowned everything else in the ears of the pilot.

The luckless man tried to make a sharp turn, to get out of danger. One of his wing tips caught on the canvas tent, or hangar, and in another instant there was a crash and a mass of wreckage. From this, a little later, poor Parla was carried.

But the others did not stay, for though the shadow of death hovered over the Escadrille, the business of war went on.

After three days Tom and Jack could not stand it any longer. They begged for permission to go up into the air. It was granted, though officially they were still on leave. Ascending together in a Caudron, on a photographing assignment, they were attacked by two swift German Fokkers.

Tom worked the gun, and to such good effect that he smashed one machine, sending it down with a crash, and drove the second off. So other laurels were added to those the boys already had.

"If this keeps on we'll be soon wearing the chevrons of sergeants," said Jack, as they landed.

"Well, I'd almost give up hope of them to hear from dad," announced Tom. "I'm going to see if some word hasn't come."

But there was no message. Still the strange silence continued, and Tom and his chum did not know whether Mr. Raymond had reached Paris or not. Through his own captain, Tom appealed to the highest authority at the Escadrille, asking that a last imploring message be sent to the address in the Rue Lafayette.

This was done, and then followed another day of waiting. At last Tom said:

"Jack, I can't stand it any longer! This suspense is fierce!"

"But what are you going to do about it?"

"I'm going to Paris! That's what! We'll go there and find my father if he has arrived. If he hasn't—well, there is still some hope."

"Go to Paris!" murmured Jack.

"Yes. It's the only place where I can make uncertainty a certainty. Come on, we'll go to Paris!"

CHAPTER IV

SUSPICIONS

Tom Raymond started across the field toward headquarters. Jack followed, but there was a strange look on the latter's face.

"I don't see how you're going to Paris," remarked Jack, at length. "Do you mean we're to go in separate machines, or together?"

"Oh, nothing like that!" exclaimed Tom. "We won't go in machines at all. We'll go by train, if we can get one, or by motor."

"But you're heading for the Escadrille Headquarters office, and—"

"We've got to get official permission to go," explained Tom. "We can't rush off, whenever we like, as we used to go fishing together."

To his captain Tom explained matters more fully than he had done before. In effect he related the fact of having received the letter, stating that Mr. Raymond had started for Paris, presumably to engage in some work for the French government, or at least for the Allies. Whether he had arrived or not, and, in the former case, to ascertain why he had not sent some word to his son, was the object of Tom's quest.

"I've tried and tried, from this end, to get in touch with him," explained Tom; "but something seems to happen to my messages. I know they leave here all right, but after that they are lost. Now I have an idea that there is so much going on in Paris—so much necessary war work—that the ordinary lines of communication are choked. But if I could go to the capital in person I could soon find out whether my father was at the address he gave."

"And you want, do you, to go together?" asked the kindly French captain, smiling at Tom and Jack.

"We'd like to go," said Tom.

"And go you shall. I will write the necessary order. You have done well, and I understand you have some days of leave coming. To them I shall add more. But come back to me," he added, as he filled out the pass form. "Come back. We need you Americans now more than ever!"

"We'll come back," promised Tom. "All I want to go to Paris for is to find out about my father."

"Ah, I envy you," said the captain softly. "Both in the possession of a father, who must be proud to have such a son as you, and also because you are going to Paris. It is the most beautiful—the most wonderful—city in the world. And to think—to think that those barbarians would sack her! Ah, it is terrible!" and with a sad nodding of his head, following the shaking of an avenging fist toward the German lines, he waved Tom and Jack an adieu.

The two Air Service boys lost little time in making their preparations to leave for the French capital. They had to get certain passes and papers, and they wished to say good-bye to some of their comrades in arms. For, more than any other branch of the service, is aviation uncertain as to life or death. Tom and Jack well knew that some, perhaps many, of those who wished them "au revoir," and "bonne chance," would not be alive when they returned. And Tom and Jack might not return themselves. True, their chances were comparatively good, but the fortunes of war are uncertain.

And so, after certain preliminaries, Tom and Jack, their pet machines in the hangars, left behind their beloved comrades and were taken by motor to the nearest railway station. There they secured their tickets and took their places to wait, with what patience they could, their arrival in Paris.

The train was well filled with "permissionnaires," or soldiers on leave for a few days of happiness in the capital, and at certain stations, where more got on, the rush was not unlike that at a crowded hour in some big city.

"I see something good," remarked Jack, as they sat looking out at the scenery, glad, even for a brief moment, to be beyond the horrors of war.

"What?" asked his companion.

"There's a dining-car on this train. We sha'n't starve."

"Good enough, I almost forgot about eating," said Tom. "Now that you speak of it, I find I have an appetite."

They ate and felt better; and it was as they were about to leave the dining-car to go back to their places, that Jack nudged Tom and whispered to him:

"Did you hear what he said?"

"Hear what who said?"

"That man just back of you. Did you have a good look at him?"

"I didn't, but I will have," said Tom, and, waiting a moment so as not to cause any suspicion that his act was directed by his chum, Tom turned and looked at the person Jack indicated. He beheld a quietly dressed man, who seemed to be alone and paying attention to no one, eating his lunch.

"Well, what about him?" asked Tom. "I don't see anything remarkable about him, except that he's a slow eater. I admit I bolt my food too much."

"No, it isn't that," said Jack in a low voice. "But don't you think he looks like a German?"

Tom took another casual glance.

"Well, you might find a resemblance if you tried hard," he answered. "But I should be more inclined to call him a Dutchman. And when I say Dutchman I mean a Hollander."

"I understand," remarked Jack. "But I don't agree with you in thinking that he may be from Holland. Of course men of that nationality have a right to go and come as they choose, where they can, but I don't believe this chap is one."

"Why not?"

"Because I heard him mutter something in German."

"Well, lots of Hollanders can speak German, I have no doubt. I can splutter a few words myself, but not enough to hurt me. I began to pick up some from the prisoners, after we had that experience with Potzfeldt, when we realized that even a little knowledge of the Hun's talk, much as we hate him, would be of service. And so you think you heard this fellow speak German?" asked Tom, as he pretended to tie his shoe lace, to make an excuse for pausing.

"I'm sure I did," said Jack.

"What did he say?"

"Something about wishing he had a plate of metzel suppe. Of course I don't guarantee that pronunciation, but—"

"Oh, it'll do," said Tom, graciously. "Well, there's nothing very suspicious in that, though. I might wish for some wienerwurst, but that wouldn't make me a German spy."

"No. But take one other thing and you'll have to admit that there is some ground for my belief."

"What's the other thing, old top?" asked Tom, in imitation of some Englishmen.

"He was making drawings of the railroad line," asserted Jack.

"How do you know?"

"I saw him. He pretended to be looking at the carte de jour, and I caught a glimpse of a sheet of paper on which he was making certain marks. I'm sure he was sketching out something about the railroad, for use, maybe, in a future air raid."

"Nonsense!" exclaimed Tom. "As a matter of fact, I don't doubt that the German secret agents know every foot of ground in and about Paris. They must have maps of this railroad the same as the French have of some of Germany's, only you've got to hand it to the Huns! They certainly went into this thing well prepared the more discredit to us, in a way. But are you sure of what you say, Jack?" he added, after a moment's thought.

"Positive! I'm sure that man is a German spy, masking as a Hollander or possibly a Swiss. He's sighing for some of his country's good cooking—though that's one of the few good things about it—and he's making some sort of a map."

Tom thought over the matter a moment. The man did not appear to notice the two chums.

"I'll tell you what we can do," Tom said. "We'll soon be in at the Gare de l'Est, and we can tip off some of the officers around there. They can follow this fellow, if they think it's worth while."

"Well, I think it's worth while," said Jack. "If that fellow isn't a spy I'm a Dutchman!"

As Jack spoke the man looked up and full at the two lads, almost as if he had heard the words.

CHAPTER V

THE BOMBARDMENT OF PARIS

"There, Jack! what did I tell you? I win! You lose, and it's me for a fine dinner at your expense! You lose! Do you hear?"

Tom Raymond, with a hearty laugh, clapped his chum on the shoulder, and seemed mirthfully excited over something. As for Jack Parmly he looked first at his chuckling comrade and then at the man he suspected of being a German spy. The latter, who had glanced keenly at the boys, with something akin to anger on his face, now was plainly puzzled.

"Do you understand?" demanded Tom in a loud voice, which attracted the attention of many in the car. But a look at the two, showing them to be Americans and, therefore, to the French mind, capable of any eccentricity, seemed to make matters right. Most of the diners resumed their meals.

"See what I mean, Jack?" went on Tom. "You lose! Understand?"

"No, I don't understand," was the low-voiced and somewhat puzzled answer.

"Then for the sake of your gasolene tank pretend that you do!" fiercely whispered Tom in his chum's ear. "Play up to my game! Don't you see that fellow's suspicious of us? He thinks we've been talking about him. I win, do you understand?"

"Oh, yes," answered Jack, and then, in a louder tone, intended to allay suspicion on the part of the suspect, he added: "You win all right, Tom! I'll buy the dinner. I didn't think the train would get in so soon! It's one on me all right!"

And then, laughing and talking in seeming carelessness, as though they had not a thought in the world but the friendly wager they had made, they went back to their coach.

"That was a narrow squeak," observed Tom. "He was getting suspicious all right, and in another moment might have made an indignant demand of the guard that we cease observing him. It might have made trouble for us. We're not members of the secret police, remember."

"Well," remarked Jack, "he might have made trouble for us, but I could do the same for him. I'd let fall a hint about the map of the railway he was sketching."

"You mean all right, Jack, but I don't believe your plan would work. If that fellow really is a German spy, which I doubt, he'd destroy the map, if he made one, the moment he thought himself in danger."

"Maybe you're right, Tom," agreed his chum, a bit dubiously. "But I certainly think there is something wrong about that man."

"Maybe you think he is Carl Potzfeldt, disguised, Jack."

"No, nothing like that. Though I wouldn't be surprised if he happened to be friendly with that sneaking spy. And, speaking of Potzfeldt, Tom, though he isn't by any means a pleasant subject, do you know we are soon to be in Paris where—"

"Where Bessie and her mother are, you mean. You're right, old chap, I haven't forgotten that, and I'll wager one chance for promotion that you haven't forgotten it either."

Jack's blush was sufficient answer to his friend.

"I couldn't quite understand what you meant, Tom, by talking so suddenly and loudly about you winning and me losing," went on Jack, as they got their baggage ready, for the train was about to enter the Paris station.

"That was camouflage, Jack, pure and unadulterated camouflage," answered Tom with a laugh. "I had to do something in a hurry to get that fellow's gaze off us, or he might have made a scene, and we don't want that. But if I had made a wager with you about the time, I'd have won, for here we are, right on the dot, which is unusual in these days, I believe."

"You said something, Tom. But what are we going to do about our spy?"

"Well, if you insist that's what he is, I think the best thing would be to notify some secret service official. There must be plenty of them around the station. Every passenger, before he leaves the station, has to have his papers stamped by the military authorities. Then's your chance to tip them off about this chap."

"I'll do it, Tom. I'm not going to lose any chances of putting German enemies out of the way."

It was about five o'clock when the train pulled into the Gare de l'Est, and the passengers, including many soldiers on leave, prepared for the joys of Paris. Tom and Jack, proceeding as did the others to the place designated for the official stamping of papers, found a chance to tell their suspicions to an officer, and to point out the man Jack suspected.

"The matter shall be attended to," said the military official, treating the information with the utmost respect, and evidently considering it of more importance than Tom imagined would be attached to it. "We are greatly indebted to you, not only because you are of our beloved aviators, but because you also think to do this for France—to protect her from enemies within as well as from those who are without. France thanks you, gentlemen!" and the aged officer saluted the two young men as though he considered them his equals.

"Well, now that's off our minds we can get down to the real business that brought us to Paris," suggested Tom. "And that's to find my father—if he's here. After that we can look up Bessie and her mother, if you like, Jack."

"Of course I'll be glad to do that, Tom, and I should think that you—"

"Oh, of a surety, yes, as a Frenchman would say. I'll be happy also, to see our friends again, but I know Bessie will consider—"

"Oh, drop it, will you?" begged Jack, for he could see that his chum was about to start to rally him about the girl.

"Then," went on Tom, "the first thing to do, in my opinion, is to get to this address in the Rue Lafayette where dad said he would make his headquarters, and see why he hasn't answered any of my messages. When I once see him, and know he's all right, I'll feel better."

"Even capable of eating that dinner you claim to have won from me?" asked Jack.

"Of course."

The two Air Service boys had the satisfaction of seeing the "tip" they gave acted on, for as they left the station they observed the officer to whom they had reported, detailing a man in plain clothes, evidently one of the secret police, to follow the man they had watched in the dining car.

"We can leave the rest to the military," said Tom. "And now let's get to where we're going."

"Hadn't we better arrange for hotel accommodations, or to stop at a pension?" asked Jack. "You know Paris is crowded now, even in war times, and we've got to stay here all night, even if we learn that your father hasn't yet arrived."

"That's so," agreed Tom. "Maybe we had better get a place to bunk first."

It would not have been an easy task had they not worn the uniforms of aviators. But once these were noted, they were welcomed with smiles, and though at the first place they applied there was no room, the proprietor busied himself to such advantage that the boys were soon settled in a big double room with a fine view of a busy section of Paris.

On every side was seen evidence of the joy and satisfaction felt at the showing made by the progress of the United States in her war programme.

The stars and stripes were seen floating from many staffs, mingled with the tricolor of France and the English union jack. That Uncle Sam had at last gotten beyond the bounds of patience with a ruthless and sneaking enemy and was making energetic warfare against him was welcome news to those who had so long borne the unequal brunt of battle.

"Americans? Ah, everything that I have is yours!" the hotel proprietor told Tom and Jack. "You have but to ask. And now come, I will show you the way to the cellar."

"But we don't care to see the cellar," remarked Tom in wonder. "No doubt it is a very fine one, monsieur," he added in his best French, which was nothing to boast of. "No doubt it is most excellent, but we don't care for cellars."

"Ah, I know, but it is for protection in case of an air raid that I show it to you. It is there we all take shelter. There have been raids, and there will be more. It is well to be prepared. It is a well-protected cellar."

"Oh, well, that's different," observed Jack. "Come on, Tom, we'd better learn the best and quickest route to the basement. No telling when we might want to use it."

They descended with the proprietor and saw that he had arranged the cellar with a false roof of beams, on top of which were sand bags. In case a bomb was dropped on the hotel or in its vicinity the cellar would offer almost certain protection.

The boys arranged for a stay of at least a week in Paris, having told the proprietor their errand to the capital. By the time they had finished their dinner they found it was too late to set out in search of Mr. Raymond, as in the changed, war-time Paris little could be done in the evening. So Tom and Jack retired to their room and their bed.

"Are you going right to the Rue Lafayette?" asked Jack of his chum, the next day.

"Yes, and if we can't get any news of him there we'll appeal to the military authorities. I have a letter of introduction to persons high in authority from our captain."

The boys hailed a taxicab and gave the chauffeur the necessary directions. They were bowling along through the beautiful streets of Paris, noting on all sides the warlike scenes, and their thoughts were busily occupied, when they suddenly became aware that something had happened.

Like a thunderbolt from a clear sky there sounded a terrific explosion, and at no great distance. The concussion shook the ground, and they could feel the taxicab tremble under the shock, while the chauffeur instantly threw on all brakes, making the machine skid dangerously.

"What is it? What's the matter?" yelled Jack.

"Airship raid most likely!" shouted Tom. "Boches are dropping bombs on Paris! Oh, where's our cellar, Jack?"

The taxicab driver jumped down and opened the door.

"You had best alight, gentlemen," he said. "You must seek shelter."

"Is it an airship raid?" asked Tom.

"No, there is not an airship in sight. No such alarm has been sounded by the police. I fear the bombardment of Paris by the Germans has begun!"

CHAPTER VI

THE RUE LAFAYETTE RUINS

Tom Raymond and Jack Parmly alighted from the taxicab more quickly than they had gotten in. The chauffeur was anxiously scanning the sky. Excited men, women and children were rushing about, and yet it was not such excitement as might be caused by the first shelling of the beautiful city. It was more, as Tom said afterward, as though the populace had been taken by surprise by a new method in the same kind of warfare, for an occasional German Zeppelin or a bombing aircraft had, before this, dropped explosives. To these the French had become as much accustomed as one ever can to such terrible means of attack.

But this was different. There was no sign of a Hun aircraft, and, as the chauffeur had said, no police warning had been sounded.

"What is it?" asked Jack.

"It is a bombardment, that is all I know," replied the taxicab driver. He spoke in French, a language which the two boys used fairly well, though, as has been said, their accent left much to be desired.

"You had best seek shelter until it is over," went on the man. "I shall do so myself." He seemed to pause suggestively, and Jack handed him some money.

"Merci," he murmured, and an instant later was careening down the street at full speed.

"He isn't losing any time," said Jack.

"No. And perhaps we hadn't better, either. Where'd that shell fall?" asked Tom.

"I don't know, but it must have been somewhere about here, judging by the noise. Look, the crowd's over that way," and he pointed to the left.

It was true. Careless of the danger of remaining in the open, men, and women, too, as well as some children, were rushing toward the place where, undoubtedly, the shell from the German gun had fallen.

"Might as well take it in," suggested Jack. "I don't want to crawl down into a cellar or a subway quite yet, even if there's one around here; do you?"

"No," answered Tom, "I don't. Go on, I'm with you."

They followed the throng, but could not resist the impulse to gaze upward now and then for a possible sight of another shell, which, they half hoped, they might observe in time to run for shelter. But of course that would have been out of the question. However, quiet succeeded the din of the explosion, which had been close to the spot where the taxicab had stopped and the boys had alighted.

Following the crowd, Tom and Jack came to a side street, and one look down it showed the havoc wrought by the German engine of death. The shell, of what kind or calibre could not be even guessed, had fallen on top of an establishment where a number of women and girls were employed. And many of these had been killed or wounded. There were heart-rending scenes, which it is not good to dwell upon. But, even in the terror and horror, French efficiency was at the fore.

Ambulances were summoned, a guard was thrown about the building, and the work of aiding the injured and tenderly carrying out the dead was begun. A vast and excited throng increased in size about the building that had been hit and there was much excitement for a time.

Tom and Jack managed to get to a place where they could get a view of the havoc wrought to the structure itself, and the first thing that impressed them was mentioned by Jack, who said:

"They didn't use a very big shell, or there wouldn't have been such comparatively slight material damage done."

"The force was mostly expended inside the building," suggested Tom.

"Even so, if it had been a big shell, the kind they fired at Verdun and Liège, there'd be a crater here big enough to put a church in. As it is, only the two top stories are wrecked."

"That's right," agreed Tom. "I wonder what sort of explosive they are using? Must have been one from a bombing aeroplane."

"No, monsieur," interrupted a gendarme who was standing near. "Pardon, for speaking," he went on, with a salute, "but there was no airship observed over Paris at all. The shell came out of the clear sky."

"But it couldn't have," insisted Jack, in reply to this policeman. "If the Germans are firing on Paris they must have some place from which to shoot their gun. Either on the ground or from an airship."

"It was not an airship," insisted the gendarme. "Excuse me for insisting this to one who is in the air service," and he pointed with pride to the uniform the boys wore, "but I have seen several air raids, and I know! There was no airship seen, or I would have blown the alarm," and he motioned to his whistle which he carried for that purpose.

"It could have come from an immense airship, so high up as to be beyond observation," suggested Jack. "That's possible. Probably the Germans didn't want to be bombarded themselves by aircraft guns here, and they flew high."

The police officer shook his head. He was not convinced.

"But, man, how else could it be?" asked Tom, in some heat. "The Huns have to rest their gun somewhere, and you—Say, Jack!" he suddenly exclaimed, his face paling slightly, "you don't suppose they have broken through, do you?"

"Through our lines about Paris? Never!" cried the police officer. "They shall not pass! Our brave soldiers have said it, and they will maintain it. They shall not pass!"

"And yet," mused Tom, as he looked at the rescue work going on, "what other explanation is there? It's a bombardment of Paris all right, by German shells. If they don't come from an aeroplane, high up, they must come—"

His words were drowned by another great concussion, but farther off. The ground trembled, but there was no sign of flying debris.

"Another!" cried the gendarme. "There goes the gun again!"

"I didn't hear any gun," observed Jack. "What we heard was the explosion of the shell. Look up, Tom, and see if there's a Hun plane in sight. If there is, pity we haven't our machines right now."

The boys carried, slung over their shoulders, powerful binoculars, and with these they swept the sky. Others about them were doing the same. By this time the most seriously injured had been carried to the hospitals, and the dead had been removed, while those only slightly hurt, as well as those in the factory not at all injured, were telling their experiences. The second explosion seemed to create great terror.

"There isn't a sign of a hostile plane," said Tom, as he swept the sky with his glasses.

"I can't see any either," observed Jack. "And yet—"

There sounded the unmistakable roar of an aircraft's propeller.

"There she is!" cried some one.

But it was one of the first of a series of French planes that had hastily ascended to search the heavens for a sight of the supposed German craft that had dropped the bombs.

"What a chance we're missing!" murmured Jack.

"Yes," agreed Tom. "But they're going to have some flight before they locate that Hun. There isn't so much as a speck in the sky except the French craft."

"Let's go and see where that other explosion was," suggested Jack, when they had observed several of the French planes scurrying to and fro over the city, climbing higher and higher in search of the enemy.

"I'm with you," announced Tom. "I wonder what dad thinks of this?"

"It'll be something new for him," said Jack. "He'll have a good chance to see how his stabilizer works, if they're using it on these planes here. And maybe he can invent a better one."

"Perhaps," returned Tom. "But, Jack, do you know I'm worried about one thing."

"I have more than that on my mind, Tom. There are mighty serious times all about us, and it's terrible to think of those poor women and girls being killed like rats in a trap. I'd just like to be in my plane, and with a full gun, and then have a go at the Hun who did this."

"So would I," agreed Tom, as they made their way out of the crowd and in the direction in which many of the populace were hurrying to go to the scene of the second explosion. "But, Jack, do you know I shouldn't be surprised to learn that the shell was not from an airship at all."

"Where would it be from then?"

"The Germans may have massed such a lot of troops at some point opposite the French lines, that they have broken through and have brought up some of their heavy guns."

Jack shook his head.

"I don't believe they could do it," he said. "You know the nearest German line is about seventy miles from Paris. If they had started to break through, and had any success at all, the news would have reached here before this. And reinforcements would be on the way. No, it can't be. There must be some other explanation."

"But what is it?" asked Tom. "They've got to get nearer than seventy miles to bombard Paris. You know that."

"I don't think I really know anything about this war," said Jack simply. "So many strange, things have happened, so many old theories have been discarded, and so many new things have been done that we don't know where we are."

"Well that's true. And yet how could the Germans get near enough to bombard Paris without some word of it coming in?"

"I don't know. But the fact remains. Now let's get to where the second shell fell. Maybe we can see a fragment of it and—"

Once again the words were interrupted by an explosion. This time it was closer and the shock was greater.

"That's the third!" cried Jack.

"Yes," added Tom, looking at his watch, "and it's just half an hour since the first one fell. That indicates they're firing every fifteen minutes. Jack, there's something weird about this."

"You're right. That last one came rather close, too. I wonder where it fell?"

A man, passing them, running in a direction away from the sound of the last explosion, heard Jack's question. He paused long enough to say; "That shell fell in Rue Lafayette. Several buildings are in ruins. Many have been killed! It is terrible!"

"Rue Lafayette!" gasped Jack. "That—"

"That's where my father is supposed to be staying!" exclaimed Tom. "Come! We must see what happened!"

CHAPTER VII

TOM'S FATHER

With anxious hearts the Air Service boys ran on. There was no need to ask their way, for they had but to follow the throng toward the scene of the most recent exhibition of the Hun's frightfulness and horror.

As they drew near the Rue Lafayette, where Mr. Raymond had said he intended to stay while in Paris, the boys were halted by an officer on the outskirts of the throng.

"Pardon, but you may not go farther," he said, courteously enough. "There is danger. We are about to sound the alarm so that all may take to shelter. The Boches are raiding Paris again."

"We know it," said Tom. "But it is no idle curiosity that takes us on."

"No?" politely questioned the policeman.

"No. I am seeking my father. He wrote to me that he would stop in the Rue Lafayette, and I have not heard from him since. I was told that the last shell fell in that street."

"It did," assented the officer, "and it demolished two houses and part of another. Many were killed and injured."

"Then I must see if my father is among them!" insisted the young aviator.

"Pardon, monsieur, it is not possible. I have my instructions, and—"

He stopped, and for the first time seemed to become aware of the uniforms worn by Tom and Jack. Then the officer saluted as though proud to do it.

"Ah," he murmured. "Of the Lafayette Escadrille! You may go where you will. Only I hope it is not into danger," he said, as he drew aside for them to pass. "Pardon, I did not at first sense who you were. France owes you much, messieurs. Keep your lives save for her!"

"We will," promised Tom, as he hurried on, followed by Jack.

They came to the head of the street they sought, and, looking down it, beheld ruins greater than they had seen before. As the officer had said, two buildings had been completely demolished, and a third partly so, the wreckage of all mingling. And amid these ruins police and soldiers were working frantically to get out the injured and remove the dead, of whom there was a sad number.

Tom's face was white, but he kept his nerve. He had been through too many scenes of horror, had been too near death too often of late, as had his chum, to falter now, even though his father might be among those buried in the wreckage caused by the German shell.

"Do you know what number your father was to stop at?" asked Jack.

"Yes, I have his letter," Tom answered. "I'm afraid, Jack, it was in one of those buildings that have been blown apart."

"No, Tom!"

"I'm afraid so. But, even at that, he may have had a chance for his life. He may have been out, or, after all, he may not have arrived yet. I'm not going to give up hope until I have to."

"That's the way to talk, old man. I'm with you to the last."

They pressed on, and populace and officers alike gave way before them as they saw the uniforms.

"We've got to help!" declared Tom. "We must pitch in, Jack, and lend a hand here. The soldiers seem to be in charge. Let's report to the commanding officer and offer our services."

"But your father?"

"That's the best way to find him if he's in those ruins. Let us help get the unfortunates out. I hope I don't find him, but I must make sure."

Making their way through the press of people, which, under order of the police and military authorities, had begun to disperse in some small measure, Tom and Jack reported to the officer in charge, giving him their names and rank, at the same time showing their papers.

"We want to help," the lads told him.

"And I ask no better," was the quick response. "There are dead and dying under that pile. They must be gotten out."

And then began heart-rending scenes. Tom and Jack did valiant work in carrying out the dead and dying, in both of which classes were men, women and children.

The German beasts were living up to the mark they had set for themselves in their war of frightfulness.

Each time a dead or injured man was reached, to be carried out for hospital treatment or to have the last sad rites paid him, Tom nerved himself to look. But he did not see his father, and some small measure of thankfulness surged into his heart. But there were still others buried deep under the ruins, and it would be some time before their bodies, dead or alive, could be got out.

As the soldiers and police worked, on all sides could be heard discussions as to what new form or manner of weapon the Germans were using thus to reach Paris. Many inclined to the theory that it was a new form of airship, flying so high as to be not only beyond ordinary observation, but to be unreachable by the type of planes available at Paris.

"If we could only find a piece of the shell we could come nearer to guessing what sort of gun fired it," remarked Tom, as the two Air Service boys rested a moment from their hard, terrible labors.

"Do you mean if it was dropped from an airship it wouldn't have any rifling grooves on it?" asked Jack.

"That's it. A bomb, dropped from an aeroplane, would, very likely, be only a sort of round affair, set to explode on contact or by a time fuse. But if it was a shell fired from a long-range gun, there might be enough of it left, after the explosion, to observe the rifling."

"There isn't a gun with a range long enough to reach Paris from the nearest German lines, unless they have broken through," said Jack.

"Well, the last may have happened; though I should think we'd have got some word of it in that case. There'd be fierce fighting if the Germans tried that, and we'd rush reinforcements out in taxicabs as the Paris soldiers went out once before."

"Do you think then," asked Jack, as they went back, after their brief respite, to their appalling labors, "that they have a gun long enough to fire from their nearest point, which is about seventy miles from this city?"

"I don't know what to think," remarked Tom. "It seems like a wild dream to speak of a gun that can shoot so far; and yet reality is over-topping many wild dreams these days. I'm going to reserve judgment. My chief concern now, though of course I'm not going to let it interfere with my work, is to find my father. If he should have been in here, Jack—"

Tom did not finish, but his chum knew what he meant, and sympathized with his unexpressed fear for the safety of Mr. Raymond.

Digging and delving into the ruins, they brought out the racked and maimed bodies, and there was more than one whose eyes were wet with tears, while in their hearts wild and justifiable rage was felt at the ruthless Germans.

Ten had been killed and nearly twice that number wounded in the third shell from the Hun cannon.

From a policeman Tom learned that one of the two buildings that had been demolished was the number given by Mr. Raymond as the place he would stay.

"The place he picked out may have been full, and he might have gone somewhere else," said Tom. "We've got to find out about that, Jack."

"That's right. I should think the best person, or persons, to talk to would be the janitors, or 'concierges,' as they call 'em here."

"I'll do that," responded Tom.

Aided by an army officer, to whom the boys had recommended themselves, not only by reason of their rank, but because of their good work in the emergency, they found a man who was in charge of all three buildings as a renting agent. Fortunately he had his books, which he had saved from the wreck.

"You ask for a Monsieur Raymond," he said, as he scanned the begrimed pages. "Yes, he was here. It was in the middle building he had a room."

"In the one that was destroyed?" asked Tom, his heart sinking.

"I regret to say it—yes."

"Then I—then it may be all up with poor old dad!" and Tom, with a masterful effort, restrained his grief, while Jack gripped his chum's hand hard.

CHAPTER VIII

WHERE IS MR. RAYMOND?

Tom Raymond, having gone through a hard school since he began flying for France, soon recovered almost complete mastery of himself. The first shock was severe, but when it was over he was able to think clearly. Indeed the faculty of thinking clearly in times of great danger is what makes great aviators. For in no other situation is a clear and quick brain so urgently needed.

"Well, I'm sure of one thing, Jack," said Tom, as they walked away from the fateful ruins. "Of those we helped carry out none was my father. He wasn't among the injured or dead."

"I'm sure of that, too. Still we mustn't count too much on it, Tom. I don't want you to have false hopes. We must make sure."

"Yes, I'm going to. We'll visit the hospitals and morgues, and talk with the military and police authorities. In these war times there is a record of everybody and everything kept, so it ought to be easy to trace him."

"He arrived all right, that's settled," declared Jack. "The agent's record proves that."

"Yes. I'd like to have a further talk with that agent before we set out to make other inquiries."

This Tom was able to bring about some time later that day. The agent informed the lad that Mr. Raymond, contrary to his expectations, had arrived only the day before. Where he had been delayed since arriving in Europe was not made clear.

"But was my father in the building at the time the shell struck here?" asked Tom. "That's what I want to know."

Of this the man could not be certain. He had seen Mr. Raymond, he said, an hour or so before the bombardment, and the inventor was, at that time, in his room. Then he had gone out, but whether he had come back and was in the house when the shell struck the place, could not be said with certainty.

But if he had been in his apartment there was little chance that he had been left alive, for the explosion occurred very near his room, destroying everything. Tom hoped, later, to find some of his father's effects.

"There is just a chance, Jack," said the inventor's son, "that he wasn't in his room."

"A good chance, I should say," agreed the other. "Even if he had returned to his room, and that's unlikely, he may have run out at the sound of the first explosion, to see what it was all about."

"I'm counting on that. If he was out he is probably alive now. But if he was in his room—"

"There would be some trace of him," finished Jack.

"And that's what we've got to find."

The police and soldiers were only too willing to assist Tom in his search for his father. The ruins, they said, would be carefully gone over in an endeavor to get a piece of the German shell to ascertain its nature and the kind of gun that fired it. During that search some trace might be found of Mr. Raymond.

It did not take long to establish one fact—that the inventor's body was not among the dead carried out. Nor was he numbered with the injured in the hospitals. Careful records had been kept, and no one at all answering to his description had been taken out or cared for.

And yet, of course, there was the nerve-racking possibility that he might have been so terribly mutilated that his body was beyond all human semblance. The place where his room had been was a mass of splintered wood and crumbled masonry. There was none of his effects discernible, and Tom did not know what to think.

"We've just got to wait," he said to Jack, late that afternoon, when their search of the hospitals and morgues had ended fruitlessly.

Meanwhile the French airmen had been scouring the sky for a sight of the German craft that might have released the death-dealing bombs on the city. But their success had been nil. Not a Hun had been sighted, and one aviator went up nearly four miles in an endeavor to locate a hostile craft.

Of course it was possible that a super-machine of the Huns had flown higher, but this did not seem feasible.

"There is some other explanation of the bombardment of Paris, I'm sure," said Tom, as he and Jack went to their lodgings. "It will be a surprise, too, I'm thinking, and we'll have to make over some of our old ideas and accept new ones."

"I believe you're right, Tom. But say, do you remember that fellow we saw in the train—the one I thought was a German spy?"

"To be sure I remember him and his metzel suppe. What about him? Do you see him again?" and Tom looked out into the street from the window of their lodging.

"No. I don't see him. But he may have had something to do with shelling the city."

"You don't mean he carried a long-range gun in his pocket, do you, Jack?" and Tom smiled for the first time since the awful tragedy.

"No, of course not. Still he may have known it was going to happen, and have come to observe the effect and report to his beastly masters."

"He'd be foolish to come to Paris and run the chance of being hit by his own shells."

"Unless he knew just where they were going to fall," said Jack.

"You have a reason for everything, I see," remarked Tom. "Well, the next time we go to headquarters we'll find out what they learned of this fellow. You know we started the secret service agents on his trail."

"Yes, I know. Well, I was just sort of wondering if he had anything to do with the bombardment of Paris. You've got to look for German spies now, even under your bed at night."

The boys felt they could do nothing more that day toward finding Mr. Raymond. A more detailed and careful search of the ruins might reveal something. Until this was accomplished nothing could be done.

They ate a late supper, without much in the way of appetites, it must be confessed, and then went out in the streets of Paris. There seemed to be few signs of war, aside from the many soldiers, and even the bombardment of a few hours earlier appeared to have been forgotten. But of course there was grief in many hearts.

It was early the next morning, when Tom and Jack were getting ready to go back to the ruins in the Rue Lafayette, that, as they left their lodgings, they heard in the air above them the familiar sounds of aeroplanes in flight, and the faint popping of machine guns, to which was added the burst of shrapnel.

"Look!" cried Jack. "It's a battle in the air. The Huns are making another raid. Now we'll see how they bomb the city."

But it did not turn out to be that sort of raid. The German craft were flying low, apparently to get a view of the havoc wrought the day before. Possibly photographs were being taken.

But the French aeroplanes were ready for the foe, and at once arose to give battle, while the anti-aircraft guns roared out a stern order to retreat. It was a battle above the city and, more than once, Tom and Jack wished they could be in it.

"We'll have to get back to our hangars soon," mused Tom, as they watched the fight. "We can't be slackers, even if I can't find my father," he added bravely.

The French planes were too much for the Germans, and soon drove them back beyond the Hun lines, though perhaps not before the enemy aviators had made the observations desired.

"Well, they didn't see much," remarked Jack. "As far as any real damage was done to Paris it doesn't count, from a military standpoint."

"No, you're right," agreed Tom. "Of course they have killed some noncombatants, but that seems to be the Boche's principal form of amusement. As for getting any nearer to the capture of Paris this way, he might as well throw beans at the pyramids. It's probably done for the moral, or immoral, effect."

And this seemed to be the view taken of it by the Paris and London papers. The method of bombardment, however, remained a mystery, and a baffling one. This was a point the military authorities wished to clear up. To that end it was much to be desired that fragments of the shell should be found. And to find them, if possible, a careful search was made, not only in the ruins of the Rue Lafayette, but at the other two places where the explosions had occurred.

In no place, however, was a large enough fragment found to justify any conclusive theories, and the Parisians were forced to wait for another bombardment—rather a grim and tense waiting it was, too.

But the careful search of the Rue Lafayette ruins proved one thing. The body of Tom's father was not among them, though this did not make it certain that he was alive. He may have been totally destroyed, and this thought kept Tom from being able to free his mind of anxiety. He dared not cable any news home, and all he could do was to keep on hoping. These were anxious days for him and Jack.

Their leave of absence had been for a week only, but under the circumstances, and as it was exceptionally quiet on their sector, they were allowed to remain longer. Tom wanted to make a more thorough search for his father, and the police and military authorities helped him. But Mr. Raymond seemed to have completely disappeared. There was no trace of him since the agent for the Rue Lafayette buildings had seen him leave his room just prior to the falling of the shell.

Jack inquired about the man he suspected of being a German spy. The secret service men had him under observation, they reported, but, as yet, he had not given them any cause to arrest him. They were waiting and watching.

Meanwhile active preparations were under way, not only to discover the source of the bombardment of Paris, but to counteract it. Extra anti-aircraft guns, of powerful calibre, were erected in many places about the city, and more airmen were summoned to the defense.

As yet there had been no resumption of the bombardment, and there were hopes that the German machine, whatever it was, had burst or been put out of commission. But on the second day of the second week of the boys' stay in Paris, once more there was the alarm and the warning-from the soldiers and police, and again came that explosion.

The bombardment of Paris was being renewed!

CHAPTER IX

VARIOUS THEORIES

Two things were at once apparent to Tom and Jack as they hurried out of their pension. One was that the people of Paris were not seeking shelter after the warnings as quickly as they had done at first, and the other was that there was evident curiosity on all sides to see just what damage would be done, and from which direction it would come. With an almost reckless disregard for their safety, if not for their lives, the Parisians fairly flocked out of doors to see the results of the Huns' bombardment. It was in vain that the police and military urged them to seek safety in cellars or the places provided.

This time only one shell fell near enough to Tom and Jack to make the explosion heard, and that was so faint as to indicate that it was some distance off. What damage had been done could only be guessed at.

"But we'll find out where it is, and go take a look," said Jack.

"Maybe it'll hit right around here if we stay," suggested his chum.

"Well, I'm not taking that chance," Jack went on. "Let's find out where it landed this time."

This they could do through their acquaintance with the military authority of the district where they were then staying. A telephonic report was at once received, giving the quarter where the shell had landed. It had fallen in one of the public squares, and though a big hole had been torn in the ground and pavement, and several persons killed and wounded, no material damage had been done. As for any military effect of the shell, it was nil.

The firing was done in the early evening hours, and Tom and Jack learned that, almost to the second, the shots were fifteen minutes apart.

There was one theory that an underground passage had been made in some manner to within a comparatively few miles of Paris, and from that point an immense mortar sent up the shells in a long trajectory.

Another theory was that traitors had let the Germans through the French lines at a certain place, so they could get near enough to Paris to bombard it.

And of course the gigantic airship theory had its adherents.

But, for a time at least, no one would admit the possibility of a gun with range sufficient to shoot into Paris from the nearest German lines. The range, sixty-odd miles, seemed too great for practical belief, however nicely it might work out in theory.

"And you must remember that the gun, if gun it is, couldn't be in the very first German line," said Tom, who had studied ordnance. "It must be at least ten miles back, to allow for sufficient protection from the French guns. That would make it shoot about seventy-two miles, and I don't believe any gun on earth could do it!"

"Neither do I," added Jack. "We've got to dope out something else. But this isn't finding your father, Tom."

"I know it, and I don't mind admitting I'm clean discouraged about him, Jack. If he's alive why doesn't he send me some word? He must know where I am, and, even if he doesn't know I'm in Paris, they would forward any message he might send to our aeroplane headquarters."

"That's right. But what are you going to do about it?"

"I hardly know. He may still be in Paris, but it's such a big city that it's hard to find him. Then, too, I'm thinking of something else."

"What's that, Tom?"

"Well, dad may not want us to know where he is."

"Why in the world would he want such a thing as that?"

"Well, he might be followed, or bothered by spies. Perhaps he has come over to do some special work for the French or English army people. Maybe a spy was after him just before the big German gun wrecked his Rue Lafayette house. He may have considered this a good chance to play dead, and that's why he doesn't send some word to me."

"That's a good theory. But it isn't very comforting."

"No, but there isn't much comfort in war times. We've got to make the best of it."

"I guess you're right, Tom. Now do you want to go look at the latest work of the Hun?"

"Might as well. The bombardment seems over for the night."

"I wonder why it is they don't fire after dark."

"Probably afraid of giving the location of their cannon away by the flashes. They'd be seen at night; but during the day, if they used smokeless powder, or a smoke screen in case they can't get smokeless powder for such a big gun, it would be hard to locate the place where the shots come from. So we're comparatively safe after dark, it seems."

Later this was not to prove to be the case, but it was when Tom spoke.

The boys went to the section of the city in which the last shells had fallen. While comparatively little damage had been done, a number of persons had been killed and injured, children among them. Some fragments of the shells were picked up, but not enough to make certain any particular theory in regard to the gun.

"But if it's a gun, where could it be placed?" queried Tom of an officer. "The Germans haven't broken through, have they?"

The French officer shook his head.

"No. And please God they will never get through," he said. "But there is a gun somewhere, I am sure of that."

"Do you mean to say within ten or fifteen miles of Paris?" Jack wanted to know.

"I can not be sure. It is true there may have been traitors. We have them to contend with as well as spies. But our line is intact, and at no point along it, near enough to it to fire into Paris from an ordinary gun, can the Germans be found."

"Then it must be an extraordinary gun," suggested Jack.

"It may well be—perhaps it is. Yet, as I said, there may have been traitors. There may be a gun concealed somewhere closer to Paris than we dream. But we shall find it, messieurs! Who knows? Perhaps you may be the very ones yourselves to locate it, for we are depending on you soldiers of the air."

And it was not long before this talk came back to Tom and Jack with impressive recollection.

And meanwhile the bombardment of Paris went on, usually during the late afternoon or early morning hours—never at night, as yet.

Yet with all the frightfulness of which the unscrupulous Huns were capable, it was impossible to dampen for long the spirits of the French. Soon they grew almost to disregard the falling shells from the hidden German gun. Of course there were buildings destroyed, and lives were lost, while many were frightfully maimed. But if Germany depended on this, as she seemed to, to strike terror to the hearts of the brave Frenchmen the while a great offensive was going on along the western front, it failed. For the people of Paris did not allow themselves to be disheartened, any more than the people of London did when the Zeppelins raided them.

Indeed one Paris paper even managed to extract some humor out of the grim situation. For one day, following the bombardment, a journal appeared with "scare" headlines, telling about eleven "lives" being lost. But when one read the account it was discovered that the lives were those of chickens.

And this actually happened. A shell fell on the outlying section and blew up a henhouse, killing nearly a dozen fowls and blowing a big hole in the ground.

There were other occasions, too, when the seemingly superhuman bombardment was not worth the proverbial candle. For the shells fell in sections where no damage was done, and where no lives paid the toll. Once a shell went through a house, passing close to an aged woman, but not hurting her, to explode harmlessly in a field near by.

And it was with such accounts as these that the Paris papers kept up the spirits of the inhabitants. Meanwhile the Germans kept firing away at quarter-hour intervals, when the gun was in action.

"I wonder if there is any chance of us getting in at the game?" questioned Jack of Tom one night.

"I shouldn't be surprised. As that officer said, they'll have to depend on the aircraft to locate the gun, I'm thinking."

"And you think we have a chance?"

"I don't see why not," replied Tom. "We've been off duty long enough. I'd like to get back behind the propeller again, and with a drum or two of bullets to use in case we sight a Hun plane. Let's go and send word to our captain that we've had enough of leave, and want to go out again."

"All right. But what about your father?"

"Well, I don't know what to say," answered Tom. "I'm about convinced that he wasn't killed, or even hurt, in any of the bombardments of Paris. But where he is I don't know. I guess, as a matter of duty to France, I'll have to let my private affairs go and—"

At that instant there sounded an explosion the character of which the two boys well knew by this time.

"The big gun again!" cried Jack.

"Yes, and they're firing after dark!" added Tom. "This may be just the chance the airmen have been waiting for—to locate the piece by the flashes. Come on out and see what's doing!"

Together they rushed from their room.

CHAPTER X

THE "DUD"

Much the same sort of scene was going on in the streets of Paris as Tom and Jack had witnessed when first the populace realized that they were under fire from a mysterious German cannon. There was the initial alarm—the warnings sounded by the police and soldiers, warnings which were different from those indicating a Zeppelin or aircraft raid, and then the hurry for cover.

But it was noticeable that not so many of the people rushed for a secure hiding place as had done so at first.

"They're not so afraid of the big gun as they were," observed Jack, as he hurried along with his chum.

"No. Though it's just as well to be a bit cautious, I think. The people of Paris are beginning to lose fear because they see that the German shells don't do as much damage as might be expected."

"You're right there, Tom," said Jack. "The shells are rather small, to judge by the damage they do. I wonder why that is?"

"Probably their gun, or guns, can't fire any larger ones such a long distance, or else their airships can't carry 'em up above the clouds to drop on the city."

"Then you still hold to the airship theory?"

"Well, Jack, I haven't altogether given it up. I'm open to conviction, as it were. Of course I know, in theory, a gun can be made that will shoot a hundred miles, if necessary, but the cost of it, the cost of the charge and the work of loading it, as well as the enormous task of making a carriage or an emplacement to withstand the terrific recoil, makes such a gun a military white elephant. In other words it isn't worth the trouble it would take—the amount of damage inflicted on the enemy wouldn't make it worth while."

"I guess you're right, Tom. And yet such a gun would make a big scare."

"Yes, and that's what the Germans are depending on, more than anything else."

"But still don't you think the French will have to do something toward silencing the gun?"

"Indeed I do! And I haven't a doubt but the French command is working night and day to devise some plan whereby the gun can be silenced."

"There go the aviators now, out to try to find the big cannon," observed Jack, as he gazed aloft.

Soaring over Paris, having hastened to take the air when the signal was given, were a number of planes, their red, white and blue lights showing dimly against the black sky. They were off to try to place the big gun, if such it was, or discover whether or not some Hun plane was hovering over the city, dropping the bombs.

As Jack and Tom hastened on, in the wake of the crowd, which was hurrying toward the place where the latest shells had fallen, again came a distant explosion, showing that the gun had been fired again.

"Fifteen-minute interval," announced Tom, looking at his watch. "They're keeping strictly to schedule."

"Night firing is new for the big gun," said Jack. "I do hope they'll be able to locate the cannon by the flashes."

"It isn't going to be easy," asserted Tom.

"Why not?"

"Because you can make up your mind if the Germans were afraid to fire the piece at night at first for fear of being discovered, and if now they are firing after dark, they have some means of camouflaging the flash. In other words they have it hidden in some way."

"Well, I suppose you're right. But say, Tom, old man! what wouldn't I give to be able to be up in the air with those boys now?" and Jack motioned to the scouts who were flitting around in the dark clouds, seeking for that which menaced the chief city of the French nation.

"I'd like to be there myself," said Tom. "And if this keeps up much longer I'm going to ask permission for us to go up and see what we can do."

"Think they'll let us?"

"Well, they can't any more than turn us down. And we've got to get at it in a hurry, too, or we'll have to report back at our regular station. We aren't doing anything here, except sit around."

"No, we must get busy, that's a fact," said Jack. "It's about time we downed some Hun scout, or broke up one of their 'circus' attacks. I've almost forgotten how a joy stick feels."

A "joy stick" is a contrivance on an aeroplane by the manipulation of which the plane is held on a level keel. If the joy stick control is released, either by accident (say when the pilot is wounded in a fight), or purposely, the plane at once begins to climb, caking its passenger out of danger.

Once the joy stick is released it gradually comes back toward the pilot. The machine climbs until the angle formed is too great for it to continue, or for the motor to pull it. Then it may stop for an instant when the motor, being heavier, pulls the plane over and there begins the terrible "nose spinning dive," from which there is no escape unless the pilot gets control of his machine again, or manages to reach the joy stick.

"Well, we'll have to get in the game again soon," said Tom. "But what do you say to taking a taxi? This explosion is farther than I thought."

Jack agreed, and they were soon at the place where the last German shell had fallen—that is as near as the police would permit.

A house had been struck, and several persons, two of them children, killed. But, as before, the military damage done was nothing. The Germans might be spreading their gospel of fear, but they were not advancing their army that way.

As Tom and Jack stood near the place where a hole had been blown through the house, another explosion, farther off, was heard, and there was a momentary flare in the sky that told of the arrival of another shell.

For a few seconds there was something like a panic, and then a voice struck up the "Marseillaise," and the crowd joined in. It was their defiance to the savage Hun.

A few shots were fired by the Germans, but none of them did much damage, and then, as though operating on a schedule which must not, under any circumstances, be changed, the firing ceased, and the crowds once more filled the streets, for it was yet early in the night.

The next morning the boys went to report, as they did each day, expecting that they might be called back to duty. They also found, after being told that their leave was still in effect, that some of the aviators who had gone up the night before, to try to locate the German gun, were on hand.

"Now we can ask them what they saw," suggested Jack.

"That's what we will," assented Tom.

But the airmen had nothing to report. They had ascended high in search of a hostile craft carrying a big gun, but had seen none.

They had journeyed far over the German lines, hoping to discover the emplacement of the gun, if a long range cannon was being used. But they saw nothing.

"Not even flashes of fire?" asked Tom.

"Oh, yes, we saw those," an aviator said. "But there were so many of them, and in so many and such widely scattered places, that we could not tell which one to bomb. We did manage to hit some, though with what effect we could not tell."

"Then the German gun is still a mystery," observed Tom.

"It is. But we shall discover it soon. We will never rest until we do!"

So more and new and different theories continued to be put forth regarding the big cannon, if such it was. Ordnance experts wrote articles, alike in London, Paris, and New York, explaining that it was possible for a cannon to be within the German lines and still send a shell into the French capital. But few believed that it was feasible. The general opinion was that the gun was of comparative short range, and was hidden much nearer Paris than the sixty or seventy-odd miles away, beyond which stretched the German line of trenches.

Meanwhile Tom, though making careful inquiries, had learned nothing of his father. He did not feel it would be wise to cable back home, and ask what the news was there.

"It might spoil dad's plans if I did that," said Tom to his chum, "and it would worry the folks in Bridgeton to know that I haven't yet seen him in France. No, I'll just have to wait."

And wait Tom did, though there is no harder task in all the world.

It was one morning, after a night bombardment on the part of the Germans, that Jack, who had been out for a morning paper, came rushing into the room where Tom was just awakening.

"Great news, old man! Great!" cried Jack, waving the paper about his head.

"You mean about a victory?" asked Tom.

"No, not exactly, though it may lead to that. And it isn't any news about your father, I'm sorry to say. It's about the German gun. A 'dud' fell last night."

"A 'dud'?" repeated Tom, hardly sensing what Jack said.

"Yes, you know! A shell that didn't explode. Now they have a whole one to examine, and they can find out what sort of gun shot it. This paper tells all about it. Come on! Let's go for a look at the 'dud'!"

CHAPTER XI

A MONSTER CANNON

Tom, dressing hastily, read the account in the Paris paper of the fall, in an outlying section of the city, of one of the German shells that failed to explode. It was being examined by the military authorities, it was stated, with a view to finding out what sort of gun fired it, so that measures might be taken to blow up the piece or render it useless to the enemy.

"That sounds good to me," said Tom, as they made a hasty breakfast. "This is getting down to a scientific basis. An unexploded shell ought to give 'em a line on the kind of gun that fired it."

"The only trouble," said Jack, "is that the shell may go off when they are examining it."

"Oh, trust the French ordnance experts not to let a thing like that happen," said Tom. "Now let's go to it."

It was fortunate that Tom and Jack wore the uniforms that had so endeared them to France, or they might have had difficulty in gaining admittance to the bureau where the unexploded shell was under process of investigation. But when they first applied, their request was referred to a grizzled veteran who smiled kindly at them, patted them on the shoulders, called them the saviors of France, and ushered them into the ordnance department, where special deputies were in conference.

"Yes, we have one of the Boche shells," said an officer, who spoke English fluently, for which Tom and Jack were glad. They could speak and understand French, but in a case like this, where they wanted a detailed and scientific explanation, their own tongue would better serve them.

"And can you tell from what sort of gun it comes?" asked Tom.

"It was fired from a monster cannon," was the answer. "That is a cannon not so much a monster in bore, as in length and in its power to impel a missile nearly eighty miles."

"Can it be done?" asked Jack.

"It has been done!" exclaimed Major de Trouville, the officer who was detailed to talk to the boys "It has been done. That is the gun that has been bombarding Paris."

"But, from a military standpoint," began Tom, "is it—"

"It is utterly useless," was the quick answer. "Come, I will show you the shell."

He led them to an apartment set aside for the testing of explosives and working out ordnance problems, and there on a table, around which sat many prominent French officials, was the German shell—the "dud," as Jack had called it.

"The charge has been drawn," explained Major de Trouville, "so there is no danger. And we have determined that the manner in which shots reach Paris from a distance of from seventy to eighty miles is by the use of a sub-calibre missile."

"A sub-calibre?" murmured Tom.

"Yes. You know, in general, that the more powder you use, and the larger the surface of the missile which receives it, the greater distance it can be thrown, providing your angle of elevation is proper."

The boys understood this much, in theory at least.

"Well," went on the major, "while that is true, there is a limit to it. That is to say you could go on using powder up to hundreds of pounds in your cannon, but when you get to a certain point you have to so increase the length of the gun, and the size of the breech to make it withstand the terrific pressure of gases, that it is impracticable to go any further. So, also, in the case of the shell. If you make it too large, so as to get a big surface area for the gases of the burning powder to act upon, you get your shell too heavy to handle.

"Now of course the lighter a missile is, the farther it will go, in comparison to a heavy one with the same force behind it. But you can not get lightness and sufficient resistance to pressure without size, and here is where the sub-calibre comes in."

"In other words the Germans have been firing a shell within a shell," broke in another officer.

"Exactly," said Major de Trouville. "The Germans have evolved a big gun, that is big as regards length, to enable the missile they fire from it to gain enough impulse from the powder. But the missile would be too large to travel all the way to Paris. So they use two. The inner one is the one that really gets here and explodes."

"What becomes of the outer?" asked Jack.

"It is a sort of container, or collar, and falls off soon after the shell leaves the big gun. If you will imagine a sort of bomb shell being enclosed in an iron case, the whole being put in a gun and fired, you will better get the idea. The outer case is made in two or more pieces, and soon after it is shot out it falls away, leaving the smaller missile to travel on. But here is where the cunning of the invention comes in. The smaller missile has all the impetus given the larger one, but without its weight. In consequence it can travel through eighty miles of atmosphere, finally reaching Paris, where it explodes."

"Wonderful!" exclaimed Jack.

"And yet it is merely the adaptation of an old theory," went on the major. "We have known of the sub-calibre theory for years, but it is not practicable. So we did not try it. The cost is too great for the amount of military damage done. And this shell, as you will see, is composed of two parts, each with a separate explosive chamber, each containing, as we discovered, a different sort of explosive. In this way if one did not go off, the other would, and so set off the one that failed. It is very clever, but we shall be more clever."

"That's right!" chimed in a chorus of fellow officers.

"We'll find the gun and destroy it—or all of them if they have more than one, as they probably have," went on the major.

He showed the boys where the shell had chambers for the time fuses to work, much as in a shrapnel shell, which can be set to go off so many minutes or so many seconds after it reaches its objective point.

"And so the great question is settled by the failure of this shell to explode," went on the major. "As soon as we saw it, and noted the absence of the rifling groove marks, we knew it must have been a sub-calibre matter. The rest was easy to figure out.

"Some of us thought there might be a big airship, stationed high above the clouds, dropping bombs. Others inclined to the theory of a double shell; that is, after one had been fired from the cannon it would travel, say, half way and then explode a charge which would impel another shell toward Paris. A sort of cannon within a cannon, so to speak. But this is not so. Nor did the theory of a shell with a sort of propeller device, like that of a torpedo, prove to be right. It is much simpler—just sub-calibre work."

"And what is going to be done about it?" asked Tom. "I mean how can the monster cannon be silenced?"

"Ah, that is a matter we are taking up now," was the answer of Major de Trouville. "I fancy we shall have to call on you boys for a solution of that problem."

"On us?" exclaimed Jack.

"Well, I mean on the aircraft service. It will be their task to search out this great German cannon for us, to enable our gunners to destroy it. Or it may be that it will have to be bombed from an aeroplane."

"That's the task I'd like all right!" cried Tom, with shining eyes.

"Same here!" echoed Jack. "Do you suppose we'll get a chance?" he asked eagerly.

"You may," was the reply. "It may take all the resources of our airmen to destroy this terror of the Germans. But it will be done, never fear!"

"Vive la France!" cried his companions, and there was a cheer in which Tom and Jack joined.

And so a part of the secret was discovered. It was a monster cannon that was devastating Paris. A great gun, the construction of which could only be guessed at. But it must be destroyed! That was certain!

CHAPTER XII

FOR PERILOUS SERVICE

Tom and Jack spent some little time looking at the strange German shell. It was of peculiar construction, arranged so that the two explosive charges would detonate together or separately, according as the mechanism was set.

But in this case it had failed to work, and the shell, falling in a bed of soft sand, near some new buildings which were going up, had not been fired by concussion, as might have happened.

"And it was just French luck that it didn't go off," observed Jack.

"That's right," agreed Tom. "If they hadn't had this whole shell to examine they wouldn't know about the big gun."

So all the theories, fantastic enough some of them, about great airships hovering over the beautiful city, and dropping bombs from a great height, were practically disproved.

"Well, now that you have decided it is a big German gun, the next question is, where is it and what are you going to do about it?" observed Tom, for he and Jack had been made so much of by the French officers that they felt quite at home, so to speak.

"Ah, messieurs, that is the question," declared Major de Trouville. "First to find the gun, and then to destroy it. The first we can do with some degree of accuracy."

"How?" asked Tom.

The major went to a large map hanging on the wall of the room. It showed the country around Paris and the various lines as they had been moved to and fro along the Western front, according as the Germans advanced or retreated.

"You will observe," said the major, "that by describing an arc, with Paris as the center of the circle, and a radius of about seventy-five miles, you will include a small sector of the German trenches. Roughly speaking this arc will extend from about Hamegicourt to Condé, both within the German lines, I am sorry to say. Now then, somewhere in this arc, or perhaps back of it, the German gun is placed. Anywhere else where it would be possible for such a monster engine of war to be erected, would bring it too close to our batteries.

"So that gives us the comparative location of the gun," went on the French officer. "But the next question is not so easy to settle—how to get rid of it. As I said, I think we shall have to depend on you airmen."

"Well, we're for the job!" exclaimed Tom.

"I know you are. And it may fall to you, or to your friends. I will talk of that later."

"Have you been able to get any idea of the kind of gun it is, or why it fires at fifteen minute intervals?" asked Jack.

"We have been able to get no really reliable information save that which we deduce by our observations of this shell and from what we know of the location of our own and the German lines," the Major went on. "Up to now our airmen have not been able to penetrate far enough without being attacked, and such few as did get well over toward the Rhine could make out nothing. I have no doubt the gun is well camouflaged."

"And is it true that it doesn't fire at night because the Germans are afraid the flashes will be seen?" asked Tom.

"That may have been the reason at first, but they have fired at night, of late, so they must have some way of concealing the flashes, or perhaps setting off other flashes at the same time so as to confuse our scouts."

"It's going to be some job," murmured Jack.

"You said something," agreed his chum.

They remained talking a little longer, and some of the officers who knew the reason for Tom's visit to Paris, expressed regret that he had no information as yet about his father.

"But take heart," one told him. "He is not dead, or we should have heard of it. Of course he may have fallen into the hands of the Germans, and then we would not know for some time."

"He may have been caught," agreed Tom. "While Tuessig is out of the game on account of his injuries, he may be able to direct Potzfeldt, and that scoundrel would have good reason for trying to get revenge on us."

"Ah, yes, I heard about your rescue of the young lady and her mother," said the major. "It was a brave deed."

"Oh, any one could have done it," said Tom, modestly.

"And have you seen them since they came to Paris?" the major proceeded.

"No, but I wish we could find them!" burst out Jack, and then he blushed at his impetuosity, while Tom murmured something about "Bessie," and Jack promptly told him to hold his tongue.

"Perhaps you may meet them sooner than you expect," went on the French officer.

"Now I wonder what he could have meant by that?" asked Jack, as he and his chum went out, after a final look at the German shell. "Does he know where they are?"

"It wouldn't be surprising, seeing that Mrs. Gleason is probably in Red Cross work, and Bessie may be helping her. We should have looked them up before," went on Tom. "But what with searching for my father, and the excitement about the bombardment, I really forgot all about them."

Jack did not say whether he had or not, the chances being that he had, more than once, thought of Bessie Gleason.

During the next two days the monster cannon continued to shoot shells at intervals into Paris. Some did considerable damage, as any shell would do in a great city, and many unfortunates were killed. But there was no reign of terror such as, undoubtedly, the Boches hoped to create. Paris remained calm, and there were even jokes made about the cannon. It was called a "Bertha" and other names, the former referring to Bertha Krupp, one of the owners of the great German ordnance works.

Word was given out that the French gunners on the front were trying to reach the big gun with their missiles. But as they were firing blindly it could not be said what havoc had been wrought.

"But, sooner or later, we'll get the range, and get within striking distance," said one of the French officers. "Then we'll show them a trick or two."

"Have the aviators done anything toward trying to find the gun?" asked Tom. "I mean anything more."

"We are perfecting our plans for the flying corps," was the answer. "Perhaps you shall know more in a few days."

"Well, I hope we'll be here when the fun begins," said Tom, grimly. "We've got another extension of leave, and I'm going to ask the police now, to co-operate with the military in seeking my father."

"I think that will be a wise plan. We will give you all the help we can."

But the quest for Mr. Raymond seemed a hopeless one, and as no confirmation could be had of his death or injury, the idea gradually became fixed in the minds of Tom and Jack that he had been made a German prisoner.

"If that is so, and I can get any trace of him, I'll go over the Rhine to get him back," snapped Tom.

"And I'll go with you!" declared his chum.

It was a few days after they had inspected the German "dud," and the boys were wondering what new developments might take place, the shelling of Paris meanwhile continuing at intervals, that one evening the boys were visited in their lodgings by Major de Trouville.

"Is there any news?" eagerly asked Tom, for he guessed that the French officer would not be paying a merely social call. Those were the strenuous days when such things had passed.

"Well, yes, news of a sort," was the answer. "But what I came to find out was whether you were so taken with these lodgings that you could not be induced to move."

"To move!" exclaimed Jack.

"Yes. Have you found anything unhealthful here?"

"Why, no," replied Tom, wonderingly. "We like it here. The landlord couldn't be nicer, and we're in a good location."

"Nevertheless, I fear I shall have to ask you to change your quarters," went on the major, and by the quizzical smile on his face the boys guessed that there was something in the wind.

"Let me ask you another question," went on the French officer. "Have you been annoyed since you have been here?"

"Annoyed? How?" inquired Tom.

"By unwelcome visitors, or by strangers."

The boys thought for a moment.

"There's one chap who lives in the same building here, whom we've seen on our staircase several times," said Jack, slowly. "Once I saw him pause at our door with a key, as though he were going to enter, but he heard me coming, and, muttering that he had taken too much wine and was a bit hazy in his memory, he went on upstairs."

"I thought as much," the major said. "Was the man you speak of familiar to you?"

"No, I can't say that he was," replied Jack, and Tom nodded his acquiescence. "I never saw him before."

"Oh, yes you have," and the major smiled.

"I have? Where?"

"On the train, coming into Paris."

"You mean the German spy?" cried Jack.

"The same," answered the Frenchman. "That's just what he is, and he is spying on you. Now, in view of what is going to happen, we don't want that to go on. So I have come to ask you to change your lodgings, and I think I can take you to one that will be most agreeable to you both."

"But what does all this mean?" asked Tom. "Is there——"

"There is 'something doing' as you say so picturesquely in the United States," interrupted the major. "I have come to tell you that you are to undertake a most perilous mission!"

CHAPTER XIII

THE SPY

Tom Raymond and Jack Parmly looked first at one another and then at the major. He had been smiling at their wonderment, but he was now serious, and regarded them gravely.

"Do you mean we have to do something to help catch this spy?" asked Tom.

"I'd like a hand in that!" exclaimed Jack. "I saw him first—he's my meat!"

"Well, get him if you can, boys," said the Frenchman. "But I did not come here to talk so much about him as about yourselves. The spy is a danger and a menace, but we know him and if he goes too far we can put out our hands and drag him back.

"No, what I referred to is more dangerous than merely trying to catch a spy at his sneaking work. I will tell you." The major suddenly left his seat near the window of the boy's room, and quickly opened the door leading to the hall. The passage was empty.

"I rather thought there might be an eavesdropper," the major explained. "I was followed here, though I don't believe the spies know my mission. However, it is best to be careful. With your permission I'll pull down the shade. There may be spies stationed across the street who, with powerful glasses, might look through the window and gather something of what we say by reading our lips. It has been done."

"The Germans don't leave much untried," commented Tom. "But what is it you want us to do, if it isn't trying to trail the spy?"

The major motioned them to draw closer to him, and then, leaving the door into the hall open, so that he could note the approach of any one, he whispered:

"You are to be two members of a picked company of air scouts who are to go out, discover the big German gun, and destroy it!"

"Whew!" whistled Tom, after a moment of thought during which he and Jack exchanged quick glances.

"Well?" asked the officer. "How does that strike you? I believe that is another of your captivating terms?"

"It's all to the good!" exclaimed Jack. "What say, Tom? We'll take that on, won't we?"

"Well, I should say!" was the enthusiastic rejoinder. "When do we start to—"

"Hush!" cautioned the major. "Not so loud. Though we have taken every precaution, there may be spies unseen by us. We had better talk no more about it here."

"Then let's go to our new lodgings, if we are to move," suggested Tom. "Will it be safe to talk there?"

"I think so," the major said. "At least you will be among friends. Not that your landlord here is not a true Frenchman; but he can not control the actions of those to whom he lets lodgings. You will be better where you are going. Then you accept the mission?" he asked in another whisper.

"Sure thing!" answered Tom, while Jack nodded his assent. "The sooner the quicker!"

"I do not quite get that," the major confessed with a smile. "But I think I gather your meaning. Now if you will proceed to this address," and he handed Tom a small slip of paper, "you will find a comfortable lodging, and you will be among friends."

"How soon can we start on—on this mission?" asked Tom.

"It will be better not to refer to it directly," the officer said. "Talk as little about it as you can. But you shall go as soon as the arrangements can be made. You will be notified."

"And what about seeing our friends—Mrs. Gleason?" asked Jack.

"Are you sure its Mrs.. Gleason you want to see?" inquired Tom.

"Oh, cut it out!" advised Jack with a blush.

"You may see them soon now," the major told him with a smile. "And I hope you'll soon have good news of your father," he added to Tom.

"I hope so, too. The suspense is telling on me."

"I should think it would. Now don't leave this bit of paper about with the address of your new lodgings on. Better commit it to memory, and then destroy the sheet. We want, if possible, to prevent the spy from knowing where you have gone. I will call a taxicab for you. You can be packed soon, I suppose?" he questioned.

"Within a half hour," answered Jack. "But say, won't that spy be on the watch, and won't he learn from the taxicab driver where we have gone?"

"Not from this taxicab driver," was the smiling answer. "He is one of our best secret service men. But treat him as you would an ordinary chauffeur. You may even give him a tip, and he will not be offended," and once more the major smiled.

Tom and Jack, having made sure they remembered the address given them, destroyed the paper, and then proceeded to get ready to move. Meanwhile Major de Trouville took his departure, promising to keep in communication with the Air Service boys.

Punctual to the half hour a taxicab appeared at the door. The boys obeyed the instructions they had received, and looked out to make sure the spy was not on hand. If he was, he was well concealed, for they did not see him.

"Though I suppose he's somewhere around," said Jack.

"Well, maybe we can fool him," suggested Tom. "We're going quite on the other side of Paris."

They made sure that, as far as could be told by observation, there was no one resembling the spy around the place or in the street in front, and then got into the cab with their baggage. The chauffeur seemed not to know them, but Tom thought there was just the slightest wink of one eye, as though to indicate that the game was going well.

Their cab was driven out along the Boulevard Ragenta, past the Gare du Nord, and across the Boulevard de Rochechquart to a small street running off the Rue Ramey, and there the cab stopped in front of a small but neat-looking house.

"Quiet enough neighborhood," remarked Jack, as they got down, and Tom tipped the cabman for the benefit of any spies who might be looking.

"Yes, I guess we can get some sleep here, if the big gun doesn't keep us awake," agreed Tom.

On the way they had passed several places where the havoc of the "Bertha" was noticeable.

Tom and Jack seemed to be expected, for the porter, who came down to get their bags, did not seem at all surprised to see them. He bade them follow him, and a little later, the cab having chugged off, the boys were settled in a pleasant room, a smiling landlady coming in to see if they wanted anything, and to tell them they could have meals with her at certain hours, or they might dine out as they pleased.

"Your friends will be here shortly," she added.

"Our friends?" questioned Tom.

"Yes," with a nod and a smile. "I was told to say they would be here shortly after you arrived."

"Oh, I guess she means the major and some of the officers will come to see how we are situated, and to tell us more about—the big stunt," said Tom in English to his chum, assuming that "big stunt" would sufficiently disguise to any listening spies, if such there were, the real object that lay before them.

"I suppose that's who she means," agreed Jack, as the landlady, who gave her name as Madame Reboux, withdrew.

The boys were busy unpacking their few belongings, for they had not brought much to Paris, not intending to stay long, when they heard voices in the hall outside their room. And at the tones of a certain voice Tom and Jack started and looked at one another.

"Listen!" exclaimed Tom.

"If I wasn't afraid you'd say I was dreaming, I'd say I knew that voice!" murmured Jack.

"I'd say the same," added Tom.

"Who would you say it was?" his chum challenged.

"Well, for a starter—"

He paused, for the voice sounded more plainly now, and it said:

"Yes, this is the right place, Mother. Oh, do you think the boys are here yet?"

"It surely will be a pleasure to meet them again," said another voice, evidently that of a woman, the other having been a girl's.

"I hope they won't have forgotten us," the girl went on, and at that Jack could no longer keep quiet. He rushed to the door, opened it, and cried:

"Bessie! Is that you?"

"Oh, it's Jack! Mother, here's Jack!" cried the girl, and she and her mother were soon shaking hands with Tom and Jack.

"So, you two were the friends we were soon to see!" exclaimed Tom, as he placed chairs for Mrs. Gleason and her daughter. Or, to be exact, Tom placed a chair for the mother, while Jack got one for Bessie.

"Yes, we were told you would be here," said Bessie's mother. "We did not know you were in Paris until we received word that it would be better for us to change our lodging and come here."

"The same word we received," said Jack. "Say, it's working out mighty queer, isn't it, Tom?"

"Yes, but very satisfactorily, I should say. Things couldn't be nicer. How have you been?" he asked, for he had not seen the girl nor her mother since the sensational rescue from the perfidious Carl Potzfeldt.

"Very well indeed," answered Mrs. Gleason. "Both Bessie and I have been doing Red Cross work. But isn't that great German gun terrible? Oh, how it has killed and maimed the poor women and children! The Huns are fiends!"

"I quite agree with you," said Tom, Jack meanwhile talking to Bessie. "But it isn't doing them the military good they thought it would, and, if all goes well, it may not very long do them any service at all."

"You mean—" began Mrs. Gleason.

But just then Bessie, who had arisen to go to the window to view the street, turned back with a start, and grasped Jack's hand.

"Look! Look!" she whispered, and through the curtains she pointed to a man on the opposite side of the way.

"Do you know him?" asked Jack.

"Know him? Yes, to my sorrow."

"Who is it?" asked Tom.

"The spy!" exclaimed Jack. "The man we saw in the train, and the same fellow who tried to get into our lodgings. In spite of our precautions he has found out where we are."

"I'm not so sure of that," said Tom. "He may not be here for any particular purpose. But do you know him too, Bessie?"

"Yes," the girl answered. "He was in the château where mother and I were held prisoners by Potzfeldt. He is a tool in the pay of that spy, and a spy himself!"

"Then we ought to do something!" exclaimed Jack, and he started to rush from the room.

CHAPTER XIV

WITH COMRADES AGAIN

"Hold on! Wait a minute!" exclaimed Tom, as he caught hold of his chum. "Where are you going?"

"Out to give warning to a policeman or to some army officer about that spy!" exclaimed Jack. "We know him to be such, and now, with Bessie's word that he was with Potzfeldt, it's enough to cause his arrest."

"Yes, maybe it is," agreed Tom, who was a bit more cautious than his impetuous chum. "But if we do that we may spoil the plans of Major de Trouville. Better let matters take their course, Jack. That spy may not know we are here, and again, he may. But if he doesn't, rushing out now would be sure to give the secret away. As it is, there is a chance we may keep it."

Jack, caught midway in his impetuous rush from the room, stood reflectively. What Tom had said to him appeared to make an impression. Then Bessie added her words of advice.

"Yes, Jack," she said, "I think it would be rather rash to go out now and confront that man, or start a chase after him. I know I'm not as experienced as you two famous birdmen," she went on with a smile, "but I've been through some terrible experiences, as almost every girl has in this war zone, and I can do more thinking than I used to. Don't you think it would be wise to wait, Mother?"

"Yes, Bessie," answered Mrs. Gleason, "I do. Our good friends in the military service who told us to come here, must have had some object. Perhaps it was connected with this same man who was so unkind to us in the château, and who was certainly a tool of that man I trusted once, but never will again—Carl Potzfeldt!" and she shuddered as she thought of what she had gone through.

"Let him go," she said to Jack. "Perhaps it is just a coincidence that he is passing just as we arrive. Our departure from our last lodgings was made secretly."

"So was ours," said Tom. "And yet I don't see how that spy found us so soon."

"It is that which makes me think it is accidental," observed Mrs. Gleason. "It would be very unwise now to go out, I think."

"All right, then I'll stay in," said Jack with a smile. "Especially as I have such good company. Tell me," he went on, "are you and your mother going to board here?" he asked Bessie.

"Yes," answered Mrs. Gleason. "And though we were told we would meet friends here we could not guess it would be you brave boys."

"Spare my blushes!" laughed Tom.

"Same here," added Jack.

"But what brings you to Paris?" asked Bessie. "I thought you boys were engaging in combats above the clouds."

"We have been fighting, though not during the last two weeks," said Tom. "I had word that my father had come over here, but he never communicated with us, and we came to Paris to look him up. So far we haven't succeeded in finding him," and he gave the details of the visit of himself and his chum to the capital, telling of their first experience during the firing of the big gun.

Bessie and Jack, who seemed to have much to say to one another, peered from behind the curtains out of the window now and then, and Jack at last reported that the spy had passed on, after stopping, apparently, to purchase some fruit at a stand on the street.

"I don't believe he knew we were here," said Bessie.

"Well, it won't do to take any chances," observed Tom. "However, we were not told to remain under cover, so I suppose we can go out when we like."

"Better wait until we get some word from the major," suggested Jack, who was getting some of his chum's caution.

All decided this was best, and the boys spent the rest of the afternoon in getting their room to rights, Mrs. Gleason and Bessie doing the same in their apartment. Mrs. Gleason had temporarily been relieved from Red Cross work to recuperate, she said, as she had been under a great strain.

Toward evening Major de Trouville, or "Trouville," as he democratically liked to be called, arrived, and when told of the sight in the street of the spy, who turned out to be the same man who was one of the captors of Bessie and her mother, the officer said:

"I am not surprised. In fact I rather looked for that, and it is one reason why I wanted to get you four together so you could see the man at the same time.

"There is now no doubt as to his intentions, and the fact that he was here so soon after you arrived proves that there is a 'leak' somewhere. We suspected as much, and I think I know where it is. It is good information to have. Well, boys, did I surprise you?" he asked, smiling.

"You did, indeed, but it was a pleasant surprise," said Jack.

"But when are we going to be allowed to do something to silence that monster cannon?" asked Tom. "It's pleasant to be here, but we are not forgetting there is work to do."

"Nor would I have you forget," said the major. "A number of persons were killed to-day by fire from the long-range gun. We believe, now, that there are two or three of them, as the shots come at closer intervals. It is imperative that something be done, and so I have brought you orders."

"Good!" cried Jack.

"That sounds like business!" commented Tom.

"In regard to your father," went on the major, addressing Jack's chum, "we will be on the watch for him, or any news of him, and, no matter where you are, unless you are captured by the Germans, you shall be informed as soon as possible."

"Is there any chance of being made prisoners?" asked Jack, and it might be noted that he did not use the word "danger."

"There is always that chance for an airman," replied the major. "But when I add that it may be possible that one or both of you will take a flight over the Rhine, you can judge, with the hold Germany has on French possessions, what the danger is."

"Over the Rhine!" exclaimed Tom. "Why, that's a flight of two or three hundred miles from Paris."

"Yes, but with the new type of Italian plane which you may use, it is not impossible in a single flight," said the major. "However, we will talk of that later. Just now I have come to tell you that you are to rejoin your comrades at the Lafayette Escadrille for a time. There arrangements will be made for the perilous venture I spoke of—the silencing of the big guns that are bombarding Paris. I wish you all success, young gentlemen."

"Thanks," murmured Jack.

"We consider it an honor to be picked for such duty," added Tom. "Are any others going to be in the game?"

"Oh, yes. We shall need a picked corps of the best airmen we have, French and Americans, and it will be no easy matter then. The Germans have probably been planning this for a long time, and they, no doubt, have taken every possible precaution against surprise or failure. But with the help of you brave Americans we shall win!"

"That's right!" chimed in Bessie. "Oh, how I wish I were a man!" and she looked enviously at Jack and Tom.

The major gave Bessie and her mother some instructions in regard to their actions should the spy come back, and then told Tom and Jack to prepare to leave Paris the next night.

"Report to your former camp," he said, "and there you will find further instructions waiting for you."

"Well, then as we have to-night, our last one free, let's go to some entertainment," suggested Tom to Bessie and her mother. "We can have supper afterward—not much of a celebration, for these are war times and it won't do to rejoice too much. But we ought to commemorate this meeting somehow."

"That's right!" agreed Jack.

So they went to a little play and had supper afterward in a quiet restaurant. That is, it was quiet until a sudden explosion a few blocks away announced the arrival of another German shell from the big gun, and then there was excitement enough.

Fortunately, however, the shots did little beyond material damage, no one being killed. At the same time, however, there appeared some German planes over Paris, doubtless to observe the effect of the dropping of the long-distance shells, and naturally the French airmen went up to give them combat.

The great searchlights began to play, picking out the hostile craft, and making them targets for the machine guns of the intrepid Frenchmen, and more than one Boche never got back over his lines again, while several Frenchmen found heroes' graves on the soil they had died to defend.

"Oh, if we were only up there helping," said Tom, as he and his friends watched.

"We shall be there very soon," murmured Jack. "And it can't be any too soon for me."

The tide of battle turned in favor of the French, the Hun planes withdrawing as the fire got too hot for them. And soon after that the long-range gun ceased firing.

It was rather a "pull" for Tom and Jack to say good-bye to Bessie and her mother in Paris, but they knew they had to do their duty. Nor would Mrs. Gleason and her daughter have kept the boys back for the world. They realized that the Air Service boys were helping to make the world safe for democracy, as they themselves were doing in their way.

And so Tom and Jack, their mission to Paris, which was the discovery of Mr. Raymond, having failed, went back to the hangars, there to be welcomed by their comrades in arms.

They arrived one morning, just after some planes from a bombing expedition over the German lines returned.

"What luck?" asked Tom of a pilot with whom he had often flown.

"The best, as regards the damage we did," was the answer. "We blew up several ammunition dumps, and put one railroad center out of business for a time. But Louis didn't come back," and the man turned aside for a moment.

"You mean your brother?" asked Jack, softly.

"Yes."

"Perhaps he is only captured," suggested Tom.

"No, his machine caught fire. They got his petrol tank. It's all up with him and La Garde. But we had our revenge. We sprayed the machine that got them until there was nothing left of it. And I'm going out again to-day in a Nieuport. They'll pay a price for Louis!"

CHAPTER XV

THE PICKED SQUADRON

"All ready, Jack?"

"Just a moment, Tom. I want to go over my struts and wires to make sure everything is taut. I don't want any accidents."

"That's right. Got plenty of ammunition drums?"

"All I can carry. I've got some tracer bullets, too."

"That's good. Glad you reminded me of them. I must put in a stock. The last time I went up I wasted a drum before I got my man."

Tracer bullets for aircraft guns, it might be observed, are balls of fire which enable the pilot to see the course his machine gun bullets are taking, so he may correct his fire.

"Well, how about you now?" asked Tom, as he added these useful supplies to his ammunition.

"I guess we're ready to start," replied Jack.

They climbed into their machines, each pilot using a single-seat, swift-flying craft, equipped with a Lewis machine gun. The squadron was going out on patrol duty, and each pilot was to observe what he could behind the German lines, and come back to report—that is if he did not happen, as was too often the case, to be bagged by a German flier. The small, swift machines did not carry the wireless outfit, and no reports could be sent back to headquarters save those the pilot himself came in with.

There was a rattle and a roar as the motors of the ten machines started, and then over the ground they went, "taxi fashion," to get the necessary speed to rise into the air. A moment later all went aloft, and were headed toward the German lines.

Tom and Jack kept as close together as was safe, but it is dangerous for two aeroplanes to approach too closely. If they do, and are not under good control, there may be a suction created that will cause a collision.

"Well, I hope I get one to-day," thought Tom, as he manipulated his "joy stick," so as to send his plane up on a sharp slant. "I want to make good, and then I'll have so much better chance to get after that German gun." And the same thought was in Jack's mind.

The squadron was to remain aloft on a two-hour patrol, that is unless something should occur to make it advisable to remain up longer. The keen eyes of Tom and Jack, as well as those of their companions of the air, were searching for signs of the Hun planes. As yet none were in sight, but it would not be long before they would come out to give battle.

Whatever else may justly be said about the Germans, their airmen are no cowards, and, when conditions are favorable, they seldom decline a chance to combat above the clouds, or lower down. So it could easily be guessed that when Tom, Jack and the others found themselves over the German lines that the Boches would be out in force.

Somewhat off to the left Tom caught sight of a captive German balloon, looming through the mist, and as it is always the desire of a French flier to destroy one of these, thus preventing the observer from sending by wireless news of the Allied front, he started for this enemy. Jack saw his friend's act, and, desiring to aid, turned his machine in the same direction.

But they had not gone far before they observed a number of black specks in the sky over the German lines.

"The Huns are coming," reflected Tom. "Now for some hot work."

And it came to him, to Jack, and the others, almost before they realized it. Tom never got a chance to attack the balloon he hoped to force to descend or to set on fire, for his attention was taken up by two German machines, which, separating from the others, headed straight for him. The lad gave one glance in the direction of Jack, and noted that a single Hun craft was about to engage with his chum.

"It's a regular German circus," thought Tom, referring to the number of hostile craft. "They delight to go out in numbers."

By this time the battle in the air had begun. It was a fight above the clouds, for both the French and the German machines were flying high, and had gone up above the bunches of fleecy vapor that now hid the ground from sight.

Tom headed straight for one of the Hun machines, seeking to get above it, always a point of vantage in an air battle, and as he rushed on he realized that his machine was being hit by bullets from one of the Hun guns.

Each bullet, as it struck, made a loud noise, as it punctured the tightly-drawn linen that covered the wings. But Tom knew that his craft could stand a number of such holes, if only the struts, the supports, and the guy wires were not broken. He had no time, now, to note what Jack or his comrades were doing, for his whole attention was taken up with the two Hun machines engaging him.

One seemed to be more skillful than the other, and to this one Tom gave his attention first. He emptied a stream of bullets full into this flier's craft, noting, after the first few bad shots, which he could tell by the tracers, that he had perfect range.

Guiding his craft with one hand and his feet, Tom worked the Lewis gun with his other hand, and he had emptied a whole drum at the daring Hun before he had the satisfaction of seeing the machine crumple up. Tom's bullets had struck some part that had caused the wings to collapse, and the airman went down to earth, his craft out of control.

But matters were not to go easy with the American. The other German was now in a better position for getting Tom than the latter was for potting him, and Tom felt a stream of bullets flying around him. One chipped his gun, and another grazed his cheek, the close call making his heart stand still for a moment. But he never faltered.

"I've got to get above him," Tom thought fiercely.

He made a risky spiral turn to one side, and began to mount, seeking to get in position to fire to better advantage. It was touch and go for a while, and he felt, rather than heard, his craft receive several bullets.

"If only the gasolene tank isn't hit," thought Tom.

But good fortune in this respect was with him, and he got in a position where he could point his machine (and the gun at the same time, for this is how the guns are aimed in the single aircraft) at the Hun flier. And then Tom sent forth a rain of bullets.

For a moment they seemed to have no effect, and yet Tom knew he had shot straight. Then, even while he felt a sharp pain in one hand, showing that he had been hit, he saw the other machine start down in a spinning nose dive. That meant he was going downward head first, and at the same time spinning around like a top.

This spinning nose dive may be intentional or accidental—that is, with the machine in control, or out of control. The spinning nose dive was discovered by accident, but is now part of the regular flying features, and is often used by aviators to escape from an enemy.

It is almost impossible to hit a plane doing a spinning nose dive, and if an aviator is over his own lines he may be able to come out of it before he reaches the ground, and so be safe. Many German planes have escaped in this way, and often a French airman has thought he has sent his enemy down disabled, when, as a matter of fact, the other has merely adopted this ruse to get away.

"Well, I don't know whether I got him, or whether he got frightened and went down to fool me," thought Tom. "Anyhow they're both out of the way, and I can go after the balloon."

But Tom could not, for two reasons. One was that the wound in his hand was bleeding profusely, and he knew it ought to be attended to before he was incapacitated. Another was that the balloon was being hauled down, and as more French planes were in the air now, making a number superior to the Huns, the latter turned tail and retreated.

It was inadvisable to follow them over their own lines now, and the squadron, or what was left of it, began to retreat. Tom noted the absence of three of the French planes, and among the missing was Jack's.

"I wonder if they got him," Tom mused, his heart becoming like lead. His eyes sought the air about him, but Jack's machine, which carried a little United States flag where it could easily be seen, was not in sight.

It was impossible to get any information up in the air. Tom would have to wait until they got back to the aerodrome. And he put on speed to get there the sooner, in order to end his suspense.

"And the other brave fellows—I wonder what happened to them," mused Tom. In his worry over the fate of Jack and the others he scarcely minded the pain in his hand.

He made a good landing, but being rather weak and faint from loss of blood, he scarcely heeded the congratulations of his comrades, who had received word, by telephone from the front, of the fate of some of the Hun machines. "Where's Jack?" Tom gasped, while a surgeon was putting a bandage on his hand.

"Right here, old scout!" came the unexpected answer, and Jack himself stepped out from amid a throng of airmen. "Why didn't you wait for me?" Jack went on. "I was coming back."

"Coming back? Did you come down safely?" asked Tom, beginning to feel a little better now. Then Tom realized the futility of his question, for was not Jack there in the flesh?

"Of course I came back, old scout," was the answer. "I had hard luck, though, but I'd have gone up again if they'd only waited for me."

"What happened?" asked Tom.

"Oh, just after I potted my man—or at least sent him down out of control—I got a bullet through my gasolene tank. Luckily it didn't set the petrol on fire, but I knew I'd better not take any chances. I tried to plug up the puncture with some chewing gum, but it wouldn't work. Guess the gum they sell now hasn't as much old rubber boot stock in it as it used to have. Anyhow it was leaking like a sieve, and I had to head for our lines."

"Tough luck!" consoled Tom. Jack did not add that he had, as soon as he landed, got into another machine, and was about to go back and join his comrades when they returned, having practically won the battle above the clouds.

Congratulations were extended to the members of the squadron, who accepted their honors modestly enough, as was characteristic of them.

Then, after Tom's wound had been dressed, and he and Jack were talking over the events of the day, there came a communication from the commander of the air division in that sector. It was an order calling on certain men to report at once for special duty. A picked squadron was to be detailed for a hazardous enterprise, it was said.

"And our names are there!" cried Jack. "Tom, old man, we're going!"

"But where is it?" asked another American flier named Boughton. "What's the game?"

Knowing the secret would be safe with him Tom said:

"We're going to pot the big German cannon that's bombarding Paris!"

CHAPTER XVI

MISSING

News of the shelling of Paris by the long-range gun had, of course, been received at the aerodrome, though there had not, as yet, many details come in. Tom and Jack, as the latest arrivals from the big city, were called upon to tell all they knew, and they related their experiences in the raids, and also told about the various theories of the big gun.

"But how are we going to find it?" asked. Boughton. "It's easy enough, of course, for our squadron to go out with a lot of bombs. But where are we going to drop 'em?"

"Oh, we're to go to Paris for further instructions before starting on the quest," said Tom, who had made some inquiries about the orders concerning the picked squadron.

"And they may have discovered its location by this time," added Jack. "We know about where it is—somewhere in the sector between Hamegicourt and Condé. The rest ought to be easy."

"Not so easy as it sounds, my friends," put in a French flier. "I know that region. It is a big one; and the Germans no doubt have their gun well camouflaged. It will not be easy."

"But we'll get it!" asserted Tom.

"Naturally," said the Frenchman, as if that was all there was to it.

Tom's wound was painful, but not dangerous, though it would keep him on the ground for a day or two. Though, as a matter of fact, none of the members of the picked squadron was allowed to go aloft after the orders came detailing them for work in connection with the monster cannon. Their places were taken by others who were sent for, some being new fliers who were burning to make a name for themselves.

Besides Tom and Jack, in the picked squadron there were Boughton, another American, Cerfe and Tierse, two intrepid Frenchmen, and Haught, an Englishman, who insisted, but with little success, that his name be pronounced as though spelled "Hoo."

These six were to be depended on to find and destroy the German cannon—all of them if there were more than one, as was likely. And to this picked squadron other members would be added as need arose. All six were skillful fliers, and brave men of the air, as may easily be guessed. They were to use whatever type of machine they liked best—the single seaters, the great bombing planes, and, it was even said, one of the immense Italian fliers.

This last was a craft capable of carrying several men and a quantity of supplies and ammunition.

Very soon, then, Tom Raymond and Jack Parmly were on their way to Paris again, accompanied by their comrades, and all would soon be engaged in the difficult and perilous task of finding the new German long-range cannon.

"I suppose you'll make another attempt to find your father?" suggested Jack to his chum, as they rode in on the train.

"Indeed I shall, if I have time. I can't understand why I haven't had some word before this. There are several possible reasons, of course. If it wasn't that we know he got to Rue Lafayette I'd say his ship had been sunk 'without a trace,' as the Germans ordered in other cases. But, of course, he safely reached this side. Then he just seems to have dropped out of sight, for I can't believe he was killed when the shell from the big gun hit the house where he had taken lodging. He may have found it advisable to return home at once, for some reason, and didn't have a chance to leave any word for me, or send me any message. And perhaps he hasn't got back to America yet. Then, too, he may be in Germany, a prisoner."

"Let us hope not," said Jack, softly, and Tom echoed the wish.

Much as he wished he could devote some time to the search for his father, Tom realized that he was working under military orders, and, however dear his father was to him, the sacrifice of his personal affairs must be made. He knew he would only have time to make some brief inquiries, and then he and Jack must go with the squadron to the headquarters assigned to it, as near the location of the big German gun as possible, and there try to silence it.

The train the picked squadron was traveling on was late, and it was dusk when they alighted at the railroad station.

"Think we'll have a chance to see anything of the bombardment?" asked Boughton.

"I was going to say I hoped not," answered Tom, "for I wish the beastly gun, or guns, would blow up. But that would take away our chance to pot 'em, and I know we all want to do that. You may see something, though they don't bombard at night as often as they do by day. Of late, however, before we left, the night firing was more frequent. Possibly they have found some means of hiding the gun flashes or of letting them mingle with others along a line so the exact location of the big Bertha is a matter of doubt."

As they alighted from the train, and were about to seek some taxicabs to take them to lodgings that had been assigned them, they all became aware of the fact that something unusual was going on. Suddenly the electric lights went out, leaving the region about the station, and indeed all of Paris, in comparative darkness.

At the same time a motor fire engine rushed screeching through the streets, giving an alarm.

"What is it?" cried Boughton. "Is the big gun firing?"

"It's a Zeppelin raid! I was here once before when they had one," said the Englishman coolly. "Mind your heads, boys. Just our rotten luck not to have a machine to go up after it."

He hurried out into the open street where he could have a view of the sky, and the others followed. There was more excitement than during the bombardment of the big gun. People were rushing here and there in search of safe places, and taxicabs, with their lamps like fireflies in the darkness, were skidding hither and yon, their horns calling for a clear way.

Suddenly there was a muffled roar, at some distance off. This was followed by a hoarse murmur, as though a burst of rage from many throats at the unspeakable outrage of the Huns in killing women and children.

At the same time the anti-aircraft guns, with which Paris is so efficiently guarded, began to bark and to send their red flashes out into the blackness of the night. They were shooting at the Zeppelin, as yet unseen by the men of the picked squadron, and the gunners aimed according to instructions sent them by wireless from scouts hovering in the air above the city.

As soon as word comes from the front, about eighty miles from Paris, that a Zeppelin is on its way to raid, an elaborate system of defense is put into operation. There are some airmen above Paris all the while, frequently as many as forty on sentry duty. But when word comes of a Zeppelin raid the whole squadron, numbering close to three hundred, goes aloft. By their searchlights, aided by those on the surface, these fliers endeavor to pick up the German machine, and, too, they endeavor to get near enough to attack it.

This was what was now going on. Pandemonium appeared let loose, and the explosion of the German bombs, mingling with the noise of the French guns, made Paris seem like a battlefield. Occasionally could be heard, when the guns were silenced for a moment, the roar of the many aeroplane motors aloft.

The Zeppelin seemed to be over a section of Paris near the Tuileries, judging by the bursts of light in that direction. Tom, Jack, and their friends wished with all their hearts that they might take a hand in the defense, but it was not to be. For perhaps half an hour the anti-aircraft guns roared out their defiance to the Hun, and then a large flare of gasolene was lighted in a public square.

This was a signal for the aeroplanes to return, for the Zeppelin had left, either because she found the situation too perilous for her, or because she had used up all her bombs.

The lights were turned on again, and the new arrivals watched the aeroplanes returning one by one, being recognized by their lights in the air as they moved about like gigantic illuminated insects.

"Well, that's some excitement," observed Tom, as he and the others finally succeeded in getting cabs, and started for their destination. "I hope no one was killed."

But the bombs of the inhuman Huns had found several marks, and while the harm from a military standpoint was small, a number of persons had been killed. Some damage had been inflicted on the Zeppelin, it was said later, one brave airman saying he got near enough to spray some bullets into one of the cabins where a crowd of officers and men were working the machine.

"We will be with you a little later," said Tom to the other members of the squadron, as, having reached their lodgings, the two chums set out.

"Where are you going?"

"To call on some ladies," answered Jack, for he and Tom had planned to see Bessie and her mother.

They reached their own former stopping place, to which they had been sent by Major de Trouville, but when they inquired for the Gleasons the landlady, who remembered the boys, stared at them in surprise, and said:

"Why, Madam Gleason and her daughter are not here! They went out this morning to meet you, and have not come back!"

"To meet us?" gasped Jack.

"Yes, in answer to your note bidding them do so!"

CHAPTER XVII

SEEKING THE GUN

Tom and Jack gazed blankly at one another. The same thought was in the minds of both.

"The spy!"

"That's who did it," declared Tom. "He forged our names to a note—no hard task since neither Bessie nor her mother knows our writing very well—and he's induced them to go some place where he could get them in his power again."

"But why?" asked Jack.

"Probably because Potzfeldt wanted him to do it. He still has his eye on Mrs. Gleason's property, I presume, if there is any left after his robbery."

"It certainly is tough to think that Bessie and her mother have again fallen into his clutches!" exclaimed Jack. "And we can't do a thing to rescue them. We've got to report with the others in the morning at the new aerodrome."

"Yes, but we still have to-night free!" cried Tom. "It will give us several hours to make a search, and we'll do it! Do you know where Mrs. Gleason and Bessie went in response to this forged note?" he asked the landlady.

She mentioned a certain restaurant, not far away, where Tom and his chum had frequently eaten with Mrs. Gleason and her daughter.

"She was rather surprised to get the note from you," said the landlady, "and wondered why you didn't come yourself. But she supposed it had something to do either with your search for your father or with war matters, so she did not question the messenger. I heard her mention the place where she and Bessie were going, or I would not know."

"How long ago was it?" asked Jack.

"Oh, just before luncheon time. And they haven't come back."

"The scoundrels have a long start of us!" exclaimed Jack. "We'll have to do the best we can."

"Better notify the police at once," suggested Tom. "We'll need their help."

"That's right," agreed his chum.

Their uniform was an open sesame to the police officials, and a detective was at once detailed to go with the boys to the restaurant. There, as might have been expected, there was no news. The spy, or whoever Potzfeldt's agent was, had been too clever for that. All that could be learned from a taxicab driver was that a lady and a girl, answering the descriptions of Bessie and her mother, had been met in front of the restaurant by a man.

The three, after a short talk, had driven off together in an automobile, and that was the last seen of them.

"But we'll get some trace," declared the detective. "It is hard to get in or out of Paris now without proper papers. And while, of course, this spy may have forged documents, there is a chance that we may intercept him and help your friends. Time is against us, but we will do our best."

Tom and Jack knew that. There was nothing else to do, and so, worried as they were, they went back to their comrades. Tom made some inquiries about his father, but, as he feared, no news had come.

As may be imagined Tom and Jack did not pass a very restful night. The Zeppelin raid had set their nerves on edge, as well as those of every one else, and it could not be told when the big gun might begin firing again. Then the fact of Mrs. Gleason and Bessie being missing, and not knowing in what danger they might be, added to the boys' anxiety.

They paid a late visit to the police, hoping for news, but the spy had not been apprehended. Then they hurried back to get a little rest before starting with their comrades of the air to search for the monster gun.

While these events were transpiring, the French army intelligence department had not been idle. The officials knew how vitally necessary it was, in order not to have the morale of the people of Paris weakened, to do something to find and silence the big guns. And first it was necessary to discover them.

While this, as yet, had not been done with exactness, owing to the concealing tactics of the Germans, it was believed that the long-range cannon was hidden in a certain wood near Laon. French airmen had endeavored to spy out certain positions there, but an unusually large number of German planes had fought them off.

"That's pretty good evidence that there must be something doing," observed Tom, when he heard this information. "Laon is about ten miles behind the German lines as they exist at present. Just a breather for a good French plane. Jack, that's a trip we'll soon be taking."

"I'll be with you, old scout. How's your hand?"

"Oh, all right now. I can hold the joy stick or work the gun. I'm ready for whatever comes along."

The time had come for the picked squadron to leave Paris and assemble at the aerodrome assigned to them as their headquarters while the search for the big gun was in progress. Sad at having to leave without having some word of Mr. Raymond, and without knowing the fate of Bessie and her mother, Tom and Jack, nevertheless, bore up well and left with their comrades, going out of Paris on a train that would eventually bring them to their headquarters.

In a way their mission was a secret one. Yet it was a question if the Germans did not guess that something like what really was afoot would be undertaken in order to silence the super-cannon. They were up to all the tricks of war, and they must have realized that the French would do as the Germans themselves would do under similar circumstances.

"Well, this sure is some place!" exclaimed Tom, as they reached the camp where they were to stay until the gun had been destroyed, or until some other change in plans was necessary. "It's the best aerodrome we've struck since we began flying in this war."

"I believe you!" echoed Jack.

The place, though newly established just back of the French lines, where they opposed the German trenches, was well fitted up for the purpose to which it was to be devoted.

There were a number of canvas hangars for the aeroplanes, there were living quarters for the men, a wireless station and a well defended camp where the aviators might live in comfort during the periods between their flights.

Of course the place was open to attack by German fliers, but this was true of every place along the line. Sufficient camouflaging had been done, however, to render the spot reasonably secure from bombing. Of course a direct attack from in front would be met by the admirable French system of defense, and there were plenty of reserves that could be brought up if a general advance were attempted by the Germans. But as there was no particular place of any military or strategic importance on that sector, the worst that was to be feared was an attack from the air.

And this would be guarded against both by the French fliers themselves and by a battery of the newest type of anti-aircraft gun.

"They don't seem to have forgotten much," observed Tom, as he and Jack, with the others, went to the quarters assigned to them.

"You said something!" exclaimed Jack, admiringly.

Thus had been set up in this locality, where heretofore no aircraft activities had been carried on to any extent, a most perfect escadrille.

It was designed to destroy the big German cannon. Would it succeed?

That was a question every man of the Allies asked.

Shortly after the arrival of the picked squadron at the camp, which, in honor of Tom and Jack had been named "Lincoln," word came in over the wireless that the big gun had again fired on Paris.

"It's funny we didn't hear any report of it," said Jack.

"There have been reports enough," Tom remarked. "I've heard the booming of distant guns ever since we got near this place. Any one of them may have been the monster, or they may have been firing other guns to hide the sound of this cannon. Then, too, it may not make as much noise as we think it ought to. The Germans may have found a new kind of powder, or even some propelling gas, that makes no extraordinary report. In that case we couldn't locate the gun by the sound."

"Maybe you're right," agreed Jack. "Anyhow they're firing, that much is proved; and it's somewhere over there," and he motioned toward the German lines.

Much as the airmen desired to start at once in their search for the monster cannon, it was deemed wise to have first a consultation and a general understanding of what means should be employed.

Then, too, all the aircraft were new, having been shipped to Camp Lincoln and there assembled, and it was desired to test them before taking the dangerous flights over the German lines. So the airmen would have to spend some time—perhaps half a week—in preliminary work.

Meanwhile the great cannon would keep up its deadly, though, from a military standpoint, useless work.

And so began the preparation, if such it might be called. Every one, from the most daring "ace" to the humblest kitchen helper in the camp, was anxious for the day when it could be said that the gun was out of commission, or guns, if, as was likely, there was more than one. But the men in command knew the value of thoroughness. There must be no failure through lack of making proper plans.

But at last everything was in readiness. The planes had been tested, keyed up, and the motors run until every part of them was humming like a top. Each man felt confidence, not only in himself but in his craft, and that meant much. There were several types for the fliers to use, single-seaters, the big bombing craft, those equipped for slow flying and from which photographs were to be taken, as well as others. The taking of photographs was expected to help in revealing the position of the hidden gun.

The big Italian plane was not ready, it seemed, to be used, but it would be soon, it was said.

Then came the day and the hour when certain members of the picked squadron were to take the air to look for the gun. Tom and Jack, to their delight, were selected to go.

"What a chance!" exclaimed Jack, as he climbed into his machine, and saw that he had plenty of ammunition for the Lewis gun.

"I hope we can make good!" returned Tom.

Then they were away and up, seeking to find the monster cannon that was bringing the war into the heart of Paris.

CHAPTER XVIII

A CLOUD BATTLE

For some little time the picked squadron that was intrusted with the difficult and dangerous task of locating the big German gun flew over the French lines. Below them Tom and Jack could make out various French camps, the front and supporting lines of trenches, and various other military works. They could see a brisk artillery duel going on at one point. They noted the puffs of smoke, but of course could not hear the explosions, as their own motors were making too much noise.

Tom and Jack kept within sight of one another, and also within view of their comrades. Each plane was marked with a big number so it could be distinguished, for the aviators themselves were so wrapped in fleece-lined clothes, so attired in gauntlets, goggles and fur boots, as protection against the terrible cold of the upper regions, that one's closest friend would not recognize him at a near view.

It was the object of this first scouting expedition to make a preliminary observation over as wide a range of the enemy's country as possible. While it was hoped that the location of the big gun might be spied out, it was almost too much to expect to pick out the spot at the first trial. The Germans were keen and wary, and undoubtedly they would have laid their plans well.

"Well, I don't see any of 'em coming out to dispute our passage," thought Tom, as he looked at his controls and noted by his height gage that he was now up about two miles. "There isn't a Boche plane in sight."

And the same thing was observed by Jack and the other fliers. The Germans seemed to be keeping down, or else were higher up, or perhaps hidden by some cloud bank.

That was another hazard of the air. Going into a cloud, or above it might mean, on coming out, that one would find himself in the midst of enemies.

It is a life full of dangers and surprises. It is this which makes it so appealing to the young and brave.

On and on flew the Allied planes, and the eager eyes of the pilots were alternately directed toward the earth and then ahead of them, and upward to discern the first sight of a Hun machine, if such should venture out.

The fliers were now well over the German lines, and the batteries from below began firing at them. This was to be expected, and Tom, Jack and the others had gotten used to the bursts of shrapnel all around them. They could see the puffs of smoke where the shells burst, but they could hear no sounds.

"The 'Archies' are busy this morning," thought Jack, as he noted the firing from below, and using the French slang word for the German anti-aircraft guns.

He took a quick glance toward Tom's machine to make sure his chum, so far, was all right. Assured on this point Jack looked to his own craft.

"Well," he mused, "at this point the 'flaming onions' can't get us, but they may pot us as we go down, as we'll have to if we want to get a good view of the ground where the big gun may be hidden."

The "flaming onions," referred to by Jack, were rockets shot from a ground mortar. They have a range of about a mile, and when a series of them are shot upward in the direction of a hostile plane it is no easy matter for the aviator to pass through this "barrage." Once a "flaming onion" touches an aeroplane the craft is set on fire, and then, unless a miracle happens, the aviator falls to his death.

The German gunners, however, could not use these to advantage while the French planes kept so high up, though the shrapnel was a menace, for the Hun guns shot far and with excellent aim. A number of the scout machines were hit, Tom's receiving three bullets through the wings, while Jack's engine was nicked once or twice, though with no serious damage.

But as for the German planes they declined the combat that was offered them. Probably they had different plans in view. It soon became evident to Tom, Jack and the others that to fly at that height meant discovering nothing down below. The distance was too great. The big gun might be hidden almost anywhere below them, but until it was fired, disclosing its presence by an unusual volume of smoke, it would not be discovered. Also its fire might be camouflaged by a salvo from a protecting battery.

"It's about time he did that," said Tom to himself at last, as he noticed Cerfe, who was the leader of the air squadron, dip his plane in a certain way, which was the signal for going down. "We've got to get lower if we want to see anything," the young aviator went on. "Though they may pot some of us."

Down they went, flying comparatively low but at great speed in order to offer less of a target to the gunners below them. And, following instructions, each pilot noted carefully the section of the German trenches beneath him, and the area back of them. They were seeking the big gun.

But, though they looked carefully, it could not be seen, and finally when one of the French machines was badly hit, and the pilot wounded, so that he had to turn back toward his own lines, Cerfe gave the signal for the return.

In all this time not a Hun plane had come out to give battle. What the reason for this was could only be guessed at. It may have been that none of the German machines was available, or that skillful pilots, capable of sustaining a fight with the veterans of the French, were not on hand just then. However that may have been, Tom, Jack and the others, after firing a few rounds from their machine guns at the trenches, though without hope of doing much damage, turned back toward Camp Lincoln.

"Well, then you did not discover anything?" asked Major de Trouville, who had been transferred and given the command at Camp Lincoln.

"Nothing," answered Jack.

"If it's in the section we covered, it is well hidden," added Tom.

"And I think, don't you know," went on the Englishman, Haught, "that the only way we'll be able to hit on the bally mortar is to fly low and take photographs."

"That's my idea," said the major. "If we take a series of photographs we can develop them, enlarge them, if necessary, and examine them at our leisure. I had thought of this, but it's a slow plan, and it means—casualties. But I suppose that can't be avoided. But I wanted to try the scouting machines first.

"After all, the taking of photographs from the air of the enemy trenches and the land behind them is a most valuable method of getting information," he continued.

Men, specially trained for such observation work, examine the photographs after the aviators return with the films, and they can tell, by signs that an ordinary person would pass over, whether there is a new battery camouflaged in the vicinity, whether preparations are under way for receiving a large number of troops, or whether a general advance is contemplated. Then measures to oppose this can be started. So, Major de Trouville was right, photography forms a valuable part of the new warfare.

The photographing of the enemy positions is done in big, heavy machines, carrying two men. They must fly comparatively low, and have not much speed, though they are armed, and it takes considerable of an attack to bring them down. But of course the pilot and his observer are in danger, and, to protect them as much as possible, scout planes—the single-seat Nieuports—are sent out in squadrons to hover about and give battle to the German aircraft that come out to drive off the photographers.

"We'll undertake that," proceeded Major de Trouville. "I'll order the big machine to get ready for an attempt to-morrow at locating the gun."

"Is it still shooting?" asked Jack.

"Yes, it has just been bombarding Paris; but I have no reports yet as to the damage done."

"Aren't we doing anything at all?" asked Tom.

"Oh, yes, our batteries are keeping up a fire on the German lines along the front behind which we think the gun is concealed, but what the results are yet, we don't know."

"Well, let's hope for clear weather to-morrow," suggested Boughton.

The intervening time was occupied by the aviators in getting everything in readiness. The machines were inspected, the automatic guns gone over, and nothing left undone that could be thought of to give success.

The next day dawned clear and bright, and, as soon as it was light enough to make successful photographs, the big machine set out, while hovering above and to either side of it were several Nieuports. Tom and Jack were each occupying one of these, ready to give battle to the Huns above or below the clouds.

In order to distract the attention of the Germans as much as possible from the direct front where the airships were to cross the lines, a violent artillery fire was maintained on either flank. To this the Germans replied, perhaps thinking an engagement was pending. And so, amid the roar of big guns, the flying squadron got off.

"Now we'll see what luck we'll have," mused Tom, as he drove his machine forward, being one of the large aerial "V" that had for its angle the ponderous photographing bi-motored machine.

Over the German lines they flew, and then the Germans awoke to the necessity of ignoring the fire on their flanks and began shooting at the airships over their heads.

"This ought to bring out their pilots if they have any sporting blood," thought Jack.

And it did. The French and their allies were no more than well over German-occupied territory, before a whole German air fleet swarmed up and advanced to give battle. They flew high, intending to get above their enemies, and so in the most favorable fighting position. But Tom, Jack and the others saw this, and also began to elevate their planes.

"We certainly are going up!" mused Tom, as he noted the needle of his height gage showing an altitude of twelve thousand feet. "When are they going to stop? We're high above the clouds now."

That was true as regarded himself, Jack, and two other French planes. But still the Germans climbed. Doubtless some of them were engaging the big machine which was low down, trying to take photographs, but Cerfe and Boughton were guarding that.

"Here comes one at me, anyhow!" thought Tom, as he saw a Hun machine headed for him.

"Well, the sooner it's over the better. Here goes!" and he pressed the release of his automatic gun, meanwhile heading his craft full at the German to direct the fire, for that is how the guns are aimed in a Nieuport, the gun being stationary.

And so began the battle above the clouds.

CHAPTER XIX

QUEER LIGHTS

Tom Raymond's first few shots went wild, as he noted by the tracer bullets. Then, steering his machine with his feet, he brought it around a trifle, and, having by a quick action risen above his antagonist, he let him have a good round, full in the face. The result was disastrous to the German, for suddenly the Hun machine burst into flames, the gasolene from the punctured tank burning fiercely, and down it went a flaming torch of death.

Tom felt some bullets whistle around him, and one exploded as it struck part of his engine, but without injuring it.

"Explosive bullets, are they?" mused the young aviator. "Against all the rules of civilized warfare. Well, he won't shoot any more," he thought grimly.

But though Tom had come victorious from his engagement with his single antagonist, he had no sooner straightened out and begun to take stock of the situation, than he became aware that he was in great danger. Above him, and coming at him with the swiftness of the wind, were two speedy German machines, bent cm his destruction.

They were both firing at him, the angles of attack converging, so that if one missed him the other would probably get him.

"I've got to get out of this," Tom reasoned. He headed his plane toward the antagonist on his right, shooting upward and firing as rapidly as he could, and had the satisfaction of seeing the German swerve to one side. The fire was too hot for his liking.

The other, however, came on and sent such a burst of fire at Tom that the latter realized it was a desperate chance he was taking. He tried to get above his enemy, but the other's plane was the speedier of the two, and he held the advantage.

Tom's ammunition was running low, and he realized that he must do something. He decided to take a leaf out of the book of the Germans.

"I'll go down in a spinning nose dive," he reasoned. "They'll be less likely to hit me then. I'll have to go back, I guess, and get some more shots. I used more than I thought."

He sent his last drum at the persistent German, and, noting that the other was swooping around to attack again, went into the dangerous spinning nose dive.

The Germans may have thought they had disabled their antagonist, for this dive is one a machine often takes when the pilot has lost control. But in this case Tom still retained it, and when he had dropped out of the danger zone, he prepared to straighten out and fly back over his own lines.

It is not easy to straighten an airplane after such a dive, and for a moment Tom was not sure that he could do it. Often the strain of this nose dive, when the machine is speeding earthward, impelled not only by its propellers, but by the attraction, of gravitation, is so great as to tear off the wings or to crumple them. But after one sickening moment, when the craft seemed indisposed to obey him, Tom felt it beginning to right itself, and then he started to sail toward the French lines.

He was not out of danger yet, though he was far enough away from the two German machines. But he was so low that he was within range of the German anti-aircraft guns, and straightway they began shooting at him.

To add to his troubles his engine began missing, and he realized that it had sustained some damage that might make it stop any moment. And he still had several miles to travel!

But he opened up full, and though the missing became more frequent he managed to keep the motor going until he was in a position to volplane down inside his own lines, where he was received with cheers by his comrades of the camp.

"How goes it?" asked Major de Trouville anxiously.

"I think we are holding them off," said Tom.

He was the first one who had had to return, much to his chagrin. He leaped out of his craft, and was about to ask for another to go back and renew the battle of the clouds, when he saw the big photographing machine returning, accompanied by all but two of the escorting craft.

"A pair missing," murmured the major, as he searched the sky with his glasses.

And Tom wondered if Jack's machine was among those that had not headed back.

Eagerly he procured a pair of binoculars, and when he had them focused he identified one machine after another, at last picking out his chum's. It did not seem to be damaged.

But two of the French craft had been brought down—one in flames, the report had it, and the other out of control, and both fell within the German lines.

"Did you get any photographs of the big gun?" asked the major, when the men in the double machine had made a landing.

"We got lots of views," answered the photographer, "but what they show we can't say. As far as having seen the gun goes, we didn't spot it."

"Well, maybe the photographs will reveal it," suggested the major. "Ah, but I am sorry for the two that are lost!"

Jack's experience had been less exciting than Tom's. One machine had attacked the former, and there had been a hot engagement for a while, but the German had finally withdrawn, though to what extent he was wounded or his machine damaged Jack did not know.

However, the picked squadron had reason to feel satisfied with their efforts. All now depended on the developing of the photographs, and this was quickly done. For this part of warfare is now regarded as so important that it is possible for a plane to fly over an enemy's station, take photographs and have prints in the hands of the commanding officer inside of an hour, if all goes well.

Carefully the photographs were examined by men expert in such matters. Eagerly they looked to discover some signs of the emplacement of the big gun. But one after another of the experts shook his head.

"Nothing there," was the verdict.

"Then we've got to try again," decided Major de Trouville. "We must find that gun and destroy it!"

"Well, we're ready," announced Tom, and the others of the picked squadron nodded in assent.

And then began an organized campaign to locate the monster cannon. It continued to fire on Paris at intervals. Then three days went by without any shells falling, and the rumor became current that the gun had burst. If this had happened, there was another, or more, to take its place, for again the bombarding of the city began.

Meanwhile the air scouts did their best to find the place of the firing. Hundreds of photographs were taken, and brave scouts risked death more than once in flying low over suspected territory. But all to no purpose. Several were killed, but others took their places. Jack was hit and so badly wounded that he was two weeks in the hospital. But when he came out he was again ready to join Tom in the search.

No word came as to the whereabouts of Bessie and her mother, nor did Tom hear anything of his father. The lack of information was getting on the nerves of both boys, but they dared not stop to think about that, for the army needed their best efforts as scouts of the air, and they gave such service gladly and freely.

Every possible device was tried to find the location of the German gun, and numerous battles above the clouds resulted at different times during the scout work.

On the whole the advantage in these conflicts lay with the armies of the Allies, the Germans being punished severely. Once a German plane was brought down within the French lines, and its pilot made a prisoner.

It was hoped that some information might be gotten out of the German airman that would lead to the discovery of the big gun, but, naturally, he did not reveal the secret; and no more pressure was brought to bear on him in this matter than was legitimate. The hiding place of the gun remained a secret.

Its possible size and the nature of its shooting was discussed every day by Tom, Jack and their comrades. In order to make a cannon shoot a distance of about eighty miles it was known that it was necessary to get the maximum elevation of forty-five degrees. It was also calculated that the shell must describe a trajectory the highest point in the curve of which must be thirty-five miles or more above the earth. In other words the German cannon had to shoot in a curve thirty-five miles upward to have the missile fly to Paris. Of course at that height there was very little air resistance, which probably accounted for the ability of the missile to go so far. That, and the sub-calibre shell, made the seemingly impossible come within the range of possibility.

"What are you going to do, Tom?" asked Jack one evening, after an unsuccessful day's flight. For Tom was going toward his hangar.

"Going up."

"What for?" Jack went on.

"Oh, no reason in particular. I just feel like flying. We didn't do much to-day. Had to come back on account of mist, and we didn't see enough to pay for the petrol used. Want to come along?"

"Oh, I might, yes."

Tom and Jack went up, as did several more. But the two remained up longer than did the others, and Jack was somewhat surprised to see his chum suddenly head for the German lines, but at an angle that would take him over them well to the south of where the observation work had been carried on.

"I wonder what he's up to," mused Jack; "Guess I'd better follow and see."

There was not much chance of an aerial battle at that hour, for dusk was coming on. There had been no bombing squadron sent out, which would have accounted for Tom going to meet them, and Jack wondered greatly at his chum's action.

Still there was no way of asking questions just then, and Jack followed his friend. They sailed over the German lines at a good height, and Jack could keep Tom in view by noting the lights on his plane.

These were also seen by the Germans below, and the anti-aircraft guns began their concert, but without noticeable effect. None of the Hun airmen seemed disposed to accept a challenge to fight, so Tom and Jack had the upper air to themselves.

Below them the boys could see flashes of fire as the various guns were discharged; and at one point in the lines there was quite an artillery duel, the French batteries sending over a shower of high explosive shells in answer to the challenge from the Boches.

It was not until Jack had followed his chum back to Camp Lincoln, and they had made a landing, that a conversation ensued which was destined to have momentous effect.

"Jack, did you notice the peculiar colored lights away to the north of where we were flying?" asked Tom, as they divested themselves of their fur garments.

"You mean the orange colored flare, that turned to green and then to purple?" asked Jack.

"That's it. I thought you'd see it. I wonder what it means?"

"Oh, perhaps some signal for a barrage or an attack. Or they may have been signaling another battery to try to pot us."

"No, I hardly think so. They didn't look like signal fires. I must ask Major de Trouville about that."

"What?" inquired the major himself, who was passing and who heard what Tom said.

"Why, we noticed some peculiar lights as we were flying over the German lines in the dark. There was an orange flare, followed by a green light that changed to purple," answered Tom.

"There was!" cried the major, seemingly much excited. "You don't mean it! That's just what we've been hoping to see! Come, you must tell Laigney about this."

CHAPTER XX

THE BIG GUN

For a moment Tom and Jack did not quite know what to make of the excitement of Major de Trouville. And excited he certainly was beyond a doubt.

"You must come and tell this to Lieutenant Laigney at once," he said. "It may mean something important. Are you sure of the sequence of the colors?" he asked. "That makes all the difference."

"There was first an orange tint," said Tom, "which was followed by green and purple, the last gradually dying out."

"Orange, green and purple," murmured the major. "Can it be that for which we are seeking?"

He hurried along with the boys, seemingly forgetting, in his haste and excitement, that he was their ranking officer. But, as has been noted, the aviators are more like friends and equals than officers and men. There is discipline, of course, but there is none of the rigidity seen in other branches of the army. In fact the very nature of the work makes for comradeship.

Tom and Jack knew, slightly, the officer to whom Major de Trouville referred. Lieutenant Laigney was an ordnance expert, and the inventor of a certain explosive just beginning to be used in the French shells. It was simple, but very powerful.

"You must tell him what you observed—the strange colored lights, my boys," said the major. "By the way, I hope you carefully noted the time of the colored flares."

Tom and Jack had. That was part of their training, to keep a note of extraordinary happenings and the time. Often seemingly slight matters have an important bearing on the future.

They found Lieutenant Laigney in his quarters, making what seemed to be some intricate calculations. He saluted the major and nodded to the boys, whom he had met before.

"Lieutenant," began Major de Trouville, "these young gentlemen have something to tell you. I want you to think it over in the light of what you told me about the action of that new explosive you said the Germans might possibly be using."

"Very good, Major. I shall be delighted to be of any service in my power," was the answer.

Then Tom and Jack described what they had seen, giving the location of the colored lights as nearly as they could, and the exact time they had noted them.

"How long would it take a shell to reach Paris, fired at a distance of eighty miles from the city?" asked the major.

The lieutenant made some calculations, and announced the result of his findings.

"Then," went on the commanding officer, "if a shell was fired from the big gun, say at the moment when these two scouts observed the tri-colored fire, it should have reached Paris at seven-fifty-three o'clock."

"As nearly as can be calculated, not knowing the exact speed of the projectile, yes," answered the lieutenant.

Major de Trouville picked up the telephone and asked to be connected with the wireless station.

"Have you had any reports of the bombarding of Paris this evening?" he asked. "Yes? What time did the first, or any particular shell, arrive? Ah, yes, thank you. That is all at present."

He turned to the others, after having listened to the reply and put the instrument away.

"One of the shells exploded in a Paris street at seven-fifty-two o'clock this evening," he said.

"It beat your calculations by one minute, Lieutenant Laigney."

"Ah! Then this means—" and the younger officer seemed as excited as the major had been when Tom and Jack told him what they had seen.

"It means," finished the commanding officer, "that, in all likelihood, these young men have discovered the location of the big German cannon."

"Discovered it!" cried Jack. "Why we didn't see anything!"

"Nothing but those queer lights," added Tom.

Major de Trouville smiled at them, and Lieutenant Laigney nodded his head in assent.

"Those queer lights, as you call them," said the ordnance expert, "were the flashes of a new explosive. What the Germans call it I do not know. For want of a better name we call it Barlite, from the name of Professor Barcello, one of our experimenters, who discovered it. But a spy stole the secret and gave it to Germany. They must have managed to perfect it, though we have not used it as yet, owing to the difficulty in constructing a gun strong enough to withstand its terrific power."

"And do you mean they're using this explosive in the big German gun?" asked Jack, "And that we really saw it being fired?" cried Tom.

"That is my belief," said the lieutenant. "This explosive burns, when fired from a gun, first with an orange flame, changing to green and then to purple, as the various gases are given off."

"Those are the very colors we saw!" exclaimed Jack.

"Yes," went on Major de Trouville. "And when I heard you mention them, and when I recalled that Lieutenant Laigney had spoken of a certain explosive that gave off a tri-colored light, I suspected you had hit on the German secret."

"And do you believe we actually saw the giant cannon being fired at Paris?" asked Tom.

"Without a doubt. The time of the arrival of one of the shells coincides almost to the minute with the time that would elapse after the missile was sent on its way, and this was when you saw the queer flashes. You have discovered the area where the big gun is placed. All that is needed now are some exact observations to give us the exact spot."

"And then we can destroy it!" cried the lieutenant. "Then the menace to beloved Paris will have passed!"

"And thanks to our brave American friends!" cried the major, shaking hands with Tom and Jack. "You will win promotion for this!" he murmured.

"But the big gun isn't found yet," said Jack.

"Why, if you are right, sir," Tom said to the major, "the shells must pass right over our camp."

"They probably do. But at so far above—several miles up so as to reach the height of thirty-five—that we never know it. We neither see them nor hear them. Boys, I believe you have located the big gun! All that now remains is to destroy it!"

CHAPTER XXI

DEVASTATING FIRE

Modestly enough Tom and Jack took the new honors that came to them. As a matter of fact they were in no wise sure that they had discovered the location of the German giant cannon. It was all well enough to come in and report seeing some strange-colored flares of fire. But Tom and Jack felt that they wanted to see a thing with their own eyes before surely believing.

Of course, though, the French experts knew about what they were talking, and the major and the lieutenant seemed very sure of their ground.

"I only hope we have had the good luck to have spotted the beasts' machine," said Tom.

"You will have the honor of proving it to yourselves in the morning," Major de Trouville told them. "You shall accompany the first scouting party that goes out. We will send out two photographing machines, and enough of a squadron to meet anything the Huns can put forth. Paris shall be delivered from the Boche pests!"

"We'll do our best," said Tom, and Jack nodded in agreement.

It did not take long for the news to spread about Camp Lincoln that the two young United States aviators had, very probably, discovered by accident the big German gun.

And in telling what they had seen Tom and Jack remarked that the peculiar tri-colored fire had been in the midst of other flashes of flame, and, doubtless, smoke, but that could not be seen on account of the darkness.

"The other flashes were probably guns fired to camouflage the flash from the giant cannon, or possibly cannons," observed Major de Trouville. "But we shall see what to-morrow brings forth."

The hours of the night seemed long, but there was much to do to get ready for the next day's operations. More aviators were sent for, and the men of the air spent many hours tuning up their motors and seeing to their guns, while the big machines, which it was hoped could take pictures of the giant cannon's position, were gone over carefully.

In addition some powerful French guns were brought up—some of the longest range guns available, and it was hoped that the big aeroplanes might signal by wireless the exact location of the super-gun, so that a devastating fire could be poured on it, as well as bombs be dropped from some machines especially fitted for that work.

Camp Lincoln, where the picked squadron was situated, was in the neighborhood of Soissons, France, in a sector held by the French troops. The lines of German and French trenches, with No Man's Land in between, was about ten miles to the east of this point. This section had changed hands twice, once being occupied by the Germans, and then abandoned by them when they made the great withdrawal.

Now, perhaps ten miles back of the German trenches, the great gun was hidden, making its total distance from Paris about eighty miles, but its distance from Camp Lincoln something less than twenty miles.

Modern guns easily shoot that distance, but the commander of the forces in this section was going to shorten that. Soissons was the nearest large city to the camp. As a matter of fact the air squadron was some distance east of that place, and nearer the battleline. So that it was comparatively easy, once the location of the big gun was known, to bring up heavy artillery behind the French lines to batter away at its emplacement.

After a night of arduous labor, during which there was anxiety lest the Germans find out what was going on, morning broke, and to the relief of all it was bright.

There was an early breakfast, and then the aviators' helpers wheeled the machines from the hangars. Several big photographing craft were in readiness, and ten bombing planes were in reserve.

Major de Trouville inspected his brave men. They were as eager as dogs on the leash to be off and at the throat of the Huns. A wireless message from Paris had come in soon after breakfast, stating that nearly a score had been killed in the capital the previous night by fire from the "Bertha."

"And it's up to us to avenge them!" exclaimed Jack.

"That is what we'll do if we have any luck!" added Tom grimly.

There was a last consultation of the officers, instructions were gone over, and everything possible done to insure success. The moment a big gun was sighted, the signal was to be given and the French long-range cannon would open fire, while the bombing machines would also do their part.

"All ready! Go!" called the major, and there was a rattle and a roar that drowned his last word. The men of the air were off.

Led by Tom and Jack, the others followed. Up and up they arose, the smaller planes flying high as a protection to the more cumbersome machines of the bi-motored type. And soon the squadron, the largest that had yet ascended from Camp Lincoln, was hovering over the German lines.

The Huns seemed to realize that something more than an ordinary attack from the air was impending, for soon after the anti-aircraft guns began firing a swarm of German aviators took the air, and there was no shirking battle this time. The Huns so evidently felt the desperate need of driving away their attackers, that this, more than what the major and lieutenant had said, convinced Tom and Jack that they were at last on the track of the big gun.

Of course the two boys could not communicate with one another, but they said afterward that their thoughts were the same.

The battle of the air opened with a rush and a roar. The Germans, though outnumbered by their opponents, did not hesitate, but came on fiercely. They attacked first the big photographing planes, for they realized that these were the real "eyes" of the squadron. The impressions they received, and the views they carried back, might mean the failure of the German plans.

But the French were ready for this, and the swift little Nieuports, dashing here and there, swooping and rising, attacked the other planes vigorously.

It was give and take, hammer and tongs, fire and be fired on, smash and be smashed. It was not as one-sided a battle as it would seem it might have been owing to the superiority of numbers in favor of the French—at least at first. Several of the Allies' planes were sent down, either out of control, or in flames. But the Huns paid dearly for their quarry.

Jack and Tom ran serious risks, for the Germans, realizing that the two leading planes had some special mission, attacked them fiercely. Tom managed to shake off and disable his antagonist. But Jack's man shot with such good aim that he pierced his gasolene tank, and had it not been that Jack was able to thrust into the hole one of some wooden plugs he had brought along for the purpose, he might have had to come down within the German lines. But the wood swelled, filled the hole, and then the petrol came out so slowly that there was comparatively little danger.

And having, with some of their companions, fought their way through the German air patrol, and having escaped with minor damage to their guns, Jack and Tom looked down at the place where they had seen the queer lights.

And then, high up and at a vantage point, while below them hovered their photographing planes, the two young aviators beheld a curious sight.

In German-occupied territory, but on French soil, they saw near a railroad junction, where they were fairly well hidden in a camouflaged position, not one, but three monster Hun cannons. The guns looked more like gigantic cranes than like the accepted form of a great rifled piece of armament. The guns were so mounted that they could be run out on a small track at the moment of firing, and then propelled back again, like some of the disappearing cannon at Sandy Hook and other United States forts. Only the German guns advanced and retreated horizontally, while the usual method is vertically.

"We've discovered 'em! There they are!" cried Tom, but of course he could not hear his own voice above the roar of his motor. But he knew that he and Jack were over the very spot where the night before they had seen the colored flares from the great guns.

And they had, indeed, by a most lucky chance, located the big German guns, for there were three of them. They were placed almost midway between the railroad station of Crepyen-Lannois and the two forts known as "Joy Hills," forts which had fallen into German hands. There were two railroad spur lines from the station, and on these the heavy guns were moved to position to fire, and then run back again. Other spur lines were under course of construction, Jack and Tom, as well as the other airmen, could observe, indicating that other guns were to be mounted, perhaps to take the place of some that might be destroyed.

As a matter of fact, as was learned later, there were but two guns in service at this time, one of the three having burst.[1]

Even as the French squadron came hovering over the place where the German monster guns were placed, the advance of Tom, Jack and their comrades being disputed by the Huns, one of the super-guns was run out to fire on its specially constructed platform.

That this should be done in the very faces of the French was probably accounted for by the fact that the Germans were taken by surprise. It took some little time to arrange for firing one of the big cannons, and it was probably too late, after the French airmen were hovering above it, to get word to the crew not to discharge it.

As it happened, Tom and Jack, with Boughton, who had kept pace with them, witnessed the firing of the big gun. As it was discharged, ten other heavy guns, but, of course, of much less range, were fired off, being discharged as one to cover the report of the giant mortar. And at the same time dense clouds of smoke were sent up from surrounding hills, in an endeavor to screen the big gun from aeroplane observation. But it was too late.

In another moment, and even as the echoes of the reports of the ten cannons and the big gun were rumbling, the bombing machine of the French came up and began to drop explosives on the spot. At the same time word of the location of the great cannon was wirelessed back to the camp, and there began a devastating fire on the guns that had been, and were even then, bombarding Paris.

CHAPTER XXII

OVER THE RHINE

It was a battle of the air and on the ground at the same time. From above the French, American and British airmen were dropping tons of explosives on the emplacements of the big guns and on the railway spurs that brought them to the firing points. It might seem an easy matter for an airship flying over a place to drop an explosive bomb on it and destroy it. But, on the contrary, it is very difficult.

The bombing plane must be constantly on the move, and it takes a pretty good eye to calculate the distance from a great height sufficiently well to make a direct hit.

But a certain percentage of the bombs find their mark, and they did in this case. Tom and Jack, as well as the other scouts, looking down from their planes, saw fountains of brown earth being tossed into the air as the French bombs exploded. At the same time the photographers in the other planes were making pictures of the guns and their location.

They were hindered in this not only by the shooting of the Germans from below, who were working their anti-aircraft guns to their capacity, but by screens of smoke clouds, which were emitted by a special apparatus to hide the big guns. At the same time other cannons were being fired to disguise the sound from the immense long-range weapon, but this was of little effect, now that the location had been discovered.

Meanwhile a score or more of the Hun planes appeared in the air. They had taken flight as soon as their pilots saw the squadron of enemy machines approaching, and were eager, this time, to give battle.

"Our work's being cut out for us," murmured Tom, as he steered his machine to engage a German who seemed eager for the fray. Tom sent a spray of bullets at his enemy, and was fired at in turn. He knew his craft had been hit several times, but he did not think it was seriously damaged.

Jack, too, as he could tell by a quick glance, was also engaged with a German, but Tom had no time then to bestow on mere observation. His antagonist was a desperate Hun, bent on the utter destruction of Tom's machine. They came to closer quarters.

Down below the fighting was growing more furious. It was in the form of an artillery duel. For now the French observation machines were wirelessing back the range, and French shells were falling very near the big guns.

The heavy guns, in modern warfare, are placed miles away from the objects they wish to hit, and the only way to know where the targets are is by aeroplane observation. When the guns are ready to fire one of the artillery control planes goes up over the enemy's territory. Of course it is the object of the enemy to drive it away if possible.

But, hovering in the air, the observer in the double-motored machine notes the effect of the first shot from his side's cannon. If it goes beyond the mark he so signals by wireless. If it falls short he sends another signal. Thus the range is corrected, and finally he sees that the big shells are landing just where they are needed to destroy a battery, or whatever is the object aimed at. The observation complete, the machine goes back over its own lines—if the Germans let it.

This sort of work was going on below them while Tom, Jack and the others in the Nieuports were engaging in mortal combat with the Hun fliers. Some of the heavy French shells fell beyond the emplacements of the big guns, and others were short. The observers quickly made corrections by wireless for the gunners. Tom Raymond, after a desperate swoop at his antagonist, sent him down in flames, and then, seeking another to engage, at the same time wondering how Jack had fared, the young aviator looked down and saw one of the largest of the French shells fall directly at the side of the foremost of the three German giant cannons.

There was a terrific explosion. Of course, Tom could not hear it because of his height and the noise his motor was making, but he could see what happened. A great breach was made in the long barrel of the German gun, and its emplacement was wrecked, while the men who had been swarming about the place like ants seemed to melt into the earth. They were blotted out.

"One gone!" exclaimed Tom grimly. And then he noted that the other two guns had been withdrawn beneath the camouflage. They were no longer in sight, and hitting them was a question of chance.

Still the French batteries kept up their fire, hoping to make another hit, but it would be a matter of mere luck now, for the guns were out of observation.

The airmen observers, however, still had a general idea of where the super-weapons were, and the French gunners continued to send over a rain of shells, while the bombing machines, save one that had been destroyed by the German fire, kept dropping high explosives in the neighborhood.

"The place will be badly chewed up, at any rate," mused Tom.

He glanced in the direction where he had last seen Jack, and to his horror saw his chum's machine start downward in a spinning nose dive.

"I wonder if they've got him, or if he's doing that to fool 'em," thought Tom. As he was temporarily free from attack at that instant he started toward his friend. Hovering over him, and spraying bullets at Jack, was a German machine, and Tom realized that this fighter might have injured, or even killed, Jack.

"Well, I'll settle your hash, anyhow!" grimly muttered the young birdman to himself. He sailed straight for the Hun, who had not yet seen him, and then Tom opened fire. It was too late for the German to turn to engage his second antagonist, and Tom saw the look of hopelessness on his face as the bullets crashed into his machine, sending it down a wreck.

"So much for poor old Jack!" cried Tom.

They were well over the German lines now, and the fight was going against the French. That is, they were being outnumbered by the Hun planes, which were numerous in the air. But the French had accomplished their desperate mission. One of the German guns was out of commission, and perhaps others, while the location had been made "considerably unhealthy," as Boughton expressed it afterward.

It was time for the French to retire, and those of their machines that were able prepared to do this. But Tom was going to see first what happened to Jack before he returned to his lines.

"He may be spinning down, intending to get out of a bad scrape that way, and then straighten for a flight toward home," mused Tom. "Or he may be—"

But he did not finish the sentence.

There was but one way for Tom to be near Jack when the latter landed—if such was to be his fate—and to give him help, provided he was alive. And that was for Tom himself to go down in a spinning nose dive, which is the speediest method by which a plane can descend. But there is great danger that the terrific speed may tear the wings from the machine.

"I'm going to risk it, though," decided Tom.

Down and down he spun, and as he looked; he became aware, to his joy, that Jack had his machine under some control.

"He isn't dead yet, by any means," thought Tom. "But he may be hurt. I wonder if he can make a good landing? If he does it will be inside the German lines, though, and then—"

But Tom never faltered. He must rescue his chum, or attempt to, at all hazards.

Down went both machines, Jack's in the lead, and then, to his joy, Tom saw his friend bring the machine on a level keel again and prepare to make a landing. This was in a rather lonely spot, but already, in the distance, as Tom could note from his elevated position, Germans were hurrying toward the place, ready to capture the French machine.

"If he's alive I'll save him!" declared Tom. "My machine will carry double in a pinch, but he'll have to ride on the engine hood."

Tom was going to take a desperate chance, but one that has been duplicated and equalled more than once in the present war. He was going to descend as near Jack's wrecked machine as he could, pick up his chum, and trust to luck to getting off again before the Germans could arrive.

That Jack was once more master of his craft became evident to his friend. For the Nieuport was slowing down and Jack was making ready for as good a landing as possible under the circumstances. It was plain, however, that his machine was damaged in some way, or he would have gone on flying toward his own lines.

Tom saw his chum drop to the ground, and then saw him quickly climb out of his seat, loosing the strap that held him in. By this time other German planes were swooping toward the place, and a squad of cavalry was also galloping toward it.

"I'll beat you, though!" cried Tom fiercely.

He throttled down his engine, intending to give it just enough gas to keep it going, for he would have no one to start it for him if the motor stalled. He calculated that he could taxi the craft across the ground slowly enough for Jack to jump on and then he could get away, saving both of them.

Jack understood the plan at once. He waved his hand to Tom to show that he would be ready, and Tom felt a joy in his heart as he realized that his chum was uninjured.

Down to the ground went Tom, and he guided his machine toward Jack, standing beside his own damaged craft, waiting. Suddenly there was a sharp report, and Tom saw Jack's machine burst into flames.

"He fired into the gasolene tank!" thought Tom. "That's the boy! He isn't going to let the Huns get his machine and the maps and instruments. Good!"

Jack leaped back from the blaze that suddenly enveloped his aeroplane and then ran toward Tom's machine. As he leaped upon the engine hood, which he could do with little more risk than boarding a swiftly moving trolley car, there was a burst of rifle fire from the cavalry, some of which had reached the scene.

Jack gave a gasping cry, and fell limp. He almost slipped from the motor hood, but with one hand Tom quickly fastened his companion's life belt to the support and then, knowing Jack could not fall off, opened his engine wide.

Across the ground the double-loaded craft careened, while the cavalry opened fire.

"If they hit me now, it's all up with both of us!" thought Tom desperately.

But though the bullets splattered all around him, and some hit the machine, neither he nor Jack was struck again, nor was any vital part of the machinery damaged. Poor Jack, though, seemed lifeless, and Tom feared he had arrived the fraction of a minute too late.

Then up rose Tom's plane, up and up, the powerful engine doing its best, though the machine was carrying double weight. But the Nieuports are mechanical wonders, and once the craft was free of the earth it began climbing. Fortunately there were no swift German machines near enough to give effective chase, though some of the heavier bi-motored craft opened fire, as did the cavalry from below, as well as some of the anti-aircraft guns.

But Tom, keeping on full speed, soon climbed up out of danger, and then swung around for a flight toward his own lines. He could see, ahead of him, the fleet of French planes, going back after the raid on the big guns. Tom's plane was the rearmost one.

Then he knew that he was safe! But he feared for Jack!

One after another, such as were left of the raiding party landed. Their comrades crowded around them, congratulating them with bubbling words of joy. Yet there was sorrow for those that did not return.

"Is he dead?" asked Tom, as orderlies quickly unstrapped Jack, and prepared to carry him to the hospital. "Is he dead?"

"Alive, but badly wounded," said a surgeon, who made a hasty examination.

And then all seemed to become dark to Tom Raymond.

"Well, Jack, old man, how do you feel?"

"Oh, pretty good! How's yourself?"

"Better, now that they've let me in to see you."

"You got the big guns, I understand."

"You mean you did, too. It was as much your doings as mine. Yes, we sprayed 'em good and proper. They won't fire on Paris again right away, but I suppose they'll not give up the trick, once they have learned it. But we have their number all right. Now you want to hurry up and get well."

Jack was in the hospital recovering from several bullet wounds. They had not been as dangerous as at first feared, but they were bad enough. Tom had come to see him and give some of the details of the great raid, which Jack had been unable to hear because of weakness. Now he was convalescing.

"What's the idea of hurry?" asked Jack. "Are we going after more big cannon?"

"No, this is a different stunt now. We're going over the Rhine."

"Over the Rhine?" and Jack sat up in bed.

"Monsieur—I must beg—please do not excite him!" exclaimed a pretty nurse, hurrying up. "The doctor said he must keep quiet."

"But I want to hear about this," insisted Jack. "Over the Rhine! Say, that'll be great! Carrying the war into the enemy's country for fair!"

"I'll tell you a little later," promised Tom, moving away in obedience to an entreaty from the nurse.

CHAPTER XXIII

OFF FOR GERMANY

Whether it was Tom's news or Jack's natural health was not made clear, but something certainly caused Jack Parmly to recover strength much more rapidly then the surgeons had believed possible, so that he was able to leave the hospital soon after Tom's visit.

"And now I want you to explain what you meant by saying we were to go over the Rhine," Jack insisted to his chum. "I've been wondering and thinking about it ever since you mentioned it, but none of them would tell me a thing."

"No, I reckon not," chuckled Tom.

"Why, you old sphinx?"

"Because they didn't know. It's a secret."

"Can you tell me?"

"Sure! Because you're going to be in it if you are strong enough."

"Strong enough? Of course I'll be! Why, I'm feeling better every minute! Now you go ahead and relieve my anxiety. But first tell me—have you had any news of your father?"

Tom shook his head.

"Not a word," he answered. "I'm beginning to feel that he has been captured by the Germans."

"That's bad," murmured Jack. "And now, have you heard anything about—"

"Bessie and her mother?" finished Tom, breaking in on his chum's question with a laugh. "Yes, I'm glad I can give you good news there. They are all right, and I have a letter from Bessie for you. She wants you to come and see her."

"You have a letter? Why didn't you give it to me before? You fish!"

"It just came. And so did news about their safety."

"Then the spy didn't get 'em after all."

"Oh, yes, he got 'em all right! But he bungled the job, or rather, Bessie bungled it for him. They were rescued, and the spy was locked up. We're to go to Paris to see them. They'll tell us all about it then."

"But what has that to do with our going over the Rhine?"

"Nothing. We're to go to Paris for a rest, and to get in shape for a big effort against the Germans. I'll tell you about it."

"Forge ahead, then."

Tom got up to look at the doors and windows of the French cottage back of the lines, where Jack had been moved to complete his recovery. Tom and Jack, after the sensational raid, had been given leave of absence.

"I just want to make sure no one hears what I say, for it's a dead secret yet," Tom went on. "But this is the plan. The French have several of the biggest and newest Italian planes—planes that can carry half a dozen men and lots of ammunition. Our aerodrome is going to be shifted to the Alsace-Lorraine front, and from there, where the distance to German territory is shorter than from here, we are to go over the Rhine and bombard some of their ammunition and arms factories, and also railroad centers, if we can reach 'em."

"Good!" cried Jack. "I'm with you from the fall of the hat!"

"First you've got to build up a little," stated Tom. "There is no great rush about this Rhine-crossing expedition. A lot of plans have to be perfected, and we've got to try out the Italian plane. And, before that, we are to go to Paris."

"Who says so?"

"Major de Trouville. He's greatly pleased with the result of the raid on the big German guns, and says we're entitled to a vacation. Also he knows I want to make some more inquiries about my father. But I fear they will be useless," and Tom sighed.

"And are we to go to see Mrs. Gleason?" asked Jack.

"Yes. And Bessie, too. They'll tell us all that happened."

A few days later, having received the necessary papers, Tom and Jack were once more on their way to the capital. And this time they did not, with others, have to suffer the danger and annoyance of the long-range bombardment. It was over for a time, but there was no guarantee that the Germans would not renew it as soon as they could repair the damage done to their giant cannons.

The boys found Bessie and her mother in lodgings in a quiet part of Paris, and were met with warm greetings. Then the Gleasons told their story.

They had been inveigled out of their lodgings by the false note from the boys, and had immediately been taken in charge by the spy, who, it was proved, was an agent of the infamous Potzfeldt. But Bessie, after several days' captivity in an obscure part of the great city, managed to drop a letter out of the window, asking for help.

The police were communicated with, and not only rescued Mrs. Gleason and her daughter, but caught the spy as well, and secured with him papers which enabled a number of Germany's ruthless secret service agents to be arrested.

It was because of the necessity for keeping this part of the work quiet that no word of the rescue of Bessie and her mother was sent to the boys until after the big gun raid.

There was much to be talked about when the friends met once more, and Mrs. Gleason said she and Bessie were going back to the United States as soon as they could, to get beyond the power of Potzfeldt.

As Tom had feared, there was no news of his father, but he did not yet give up all hope.

"If he's a prisoner there's a chance to rescue him," he said.

The time spent in Paris seemed all too short, and it came to an end sooner than the boys wished. Jack was almost himself again, though he limped slightly from one of the German bullets in his leg. There was every hope, however, that this would pass away in time.

Good-byes were said to Bessie and her mother, and once more the two Air Service boys reported to their aerodrome. There they found not one, but two, of the big Italian machines, which are capable of long flight, carrying loads that even the most ponderous bombing plane would be unable to rise with.

Preparations for the bold dash into the enemy's country went on steadily and swiftly. Tom and Jack were trained in the management of the big birds of the air, and though it was essentially different from what they had been used to in the Nieuports and the Caudrons, they soon mastered the knack of it, and became among the most expert.

"I believe I made no mistake when I picked them to be part of the raiding force," said Major de Trouville.

"Indeed you did not," agreed Lieutenant Laigney. "Their work in discovering the big guns, and their help in silencing them, showed what sort of boys they are."

And finally the day came when those who were to take part in the raid across the Rhine were to proceed to a point within the French lines from which the start was to be made.

Other Italian planes would await them there, and there they would receive final instructions.

They bade farewell to their comrades in Camp Lincoln, and were given final hand-shakes, while more than one, struggling to repress his emotion wished them "bonne chance!"

This raid against one of the largest and most important of the German factory and railroad sections had long been contemplated and details elaborately worked out for it. The start was to be made from the nearest point in French-occupied territory, and it was calculated that the big Italian machines could start early in the evening, cross the Rhine, reach their objective by midnight, drop the tons of bombs and be back within the French lines by morning.

Such, at least, was the hope. Whether it would be realized was a matter of anxious conjecture.

At last all was in readiness. The final examinations of the machines and their motors had been made and the supplies and bombs were in place.

"Attention!" called the commander. "Are you ready?"

"Ready!" came from Tom, who was in command of one machine.

"Ready!" answered Haught, who was in charge of the second.

"Then go, and may good fortune go with you!"

There was a roar of the motors, and the big, ponderous machines started for Germany.

Would they ever reach it?

CHAPTER XXIV

PRISONERS

Under the evening stars, the two big Italian machines slowly, and, it must be said, somewhat ponderously, as compared with a speedy Nieuport, winged their way toward the German river, behind which it was hoped, some day, to drive the savage Huns.

"What do you think?" asked Jack of his chum, for in these latest machines, by reason of the motors being farther from the passengers, and by means of tubes, some talk could be carried on.

"I don't know just what to think," was the answer. "So much has happened of late, that it's almost beyond my thinking capacity."

"That's right. And yet I can guess one thing you have in mind, Tom, old scout."

"What is it?"

"Your father! You're hoping you can rescue him."

"That's right, I am. And as soon as this drive is over—if we come back from it with any measure of success, and I can get a long leave of absence—I'm going to make a thorough search for him."

"And I'll be with you; don't forget that!"

There was not time for too much talk of a personal nature, as Tom and Jack had to give their attention to the great plane. The motors were working to perfection, and with luck they should, within a few hours, be over the great German works, which they hoped to blow up.

Tom was in charge of the plane, but he had Jack and others to help him, and there was a certain freedom of movement permitted, not possible in even the big photographing or bombing planes.

Down below little could be seen, for they were now over the French and German trenches, and neither side was showing lights for fear of attracting the fire of the other.

But Tom and Jack had been coached in the course they were to take and, in addition, they had a pilot who, a few weeks before, had made a partially successful raid in the region beyond the Rhine, barely escaping with his life.

And so they flew on under the silent stars, that looked like the small navigating lights on other aeroplanes. But, as far as the raiders knew, they were the only ones aloft in that particular region just then. They had risen to a good height to avoid possible danger from the German anti-aircraft guns.

There was not much danger from the German planes, as, of late, the Huns had shown no very strong liking for night work, except in necessary defense.

Off to the left Tom and Jack could see the other big Italian plane, in charge of Haught. It carried only small navigating lights, carefully screened so as to be invisible from below.

"I suppose you understand the orders," said Tom, speaking to Jack.

"Well, we went over them; but it wouldn't do any harm to refresh my memory. You're to be in general charge of the navigation of the plane, and I'm to see to dropping the bombs—is that it?"

"That's it. You'll have to use your best judgment when it comes to your share. I'll get you over the German works and railroad centers, as nearly as I can in the dark, and then it will be up to you."

"I hope I don't fail," said Jack, speaking through the tube.

"You won't. Don't get nervous. Any kind of a hit will throw a scare into the Huns, and make them feel that they aren't the only ones who can make air raids. But in this case we're not bombing a defenseless town, and killing women and children. This is a fortified place we're going over, and it's well defended."

"Some difference," agreed Jack.

"And if we can get some direct hits," went on Tom, "and blow to smithereens some of their munition or armament factories, we'll be so much nearer to winning the war."

And that, in brief, was the object of the flight over the Rhine.

Once more the boys fell silent.

On and on swept the planes. Whether the Germans beneath were aware of the danger that menaced them, it is impossible to say. But they made no attempt to fire on the Italian craft. Probably because of the darkness, and owing to the great height at which they flew, the Huns were in ignorance of what was taking place.

On and on in the night and beneath the silent stars they flew. Now Tom and the pilot began watching for some landmark—some cluster of lights which would tell them their objective was within sight. But for another hour nothing was done save to guide the big craft steadily onward.

Once, as Jack looked down, he saw what seemed to be a city, and he thought this might be the place where the great factories were situated.

"No, it's an important town," Tom said, in answer to his chum's inquiries, "but it is only a town—not a fortress, as the Huns call London. That isn't fair game for us."

But half an hour later the pilot spoke sharply, and gave an order. He pointed downward and ahead and there a faint glow, and one that spread over a considerable area, could be made out.

"That is where we are to drop the bombs," said Tom to Jack.

The other machine, which had flown somewhat behind the one in which were the two chums, now swerved over at greater speed. Her pilot, too, had picked up the objective.

And now began the most dangerous part of the mission. For it would not do to drop the bombs from too great a height. There was too much risk of missing the mark. The planes must descend, and then they would be within range of the defensive guns.

But it had to be done, and the order was given. As Jack and Tom went lower, in company with the other plane, they observed that they were over a great extent of factory buildings, where German war work was going on.

And now the noise of their motors was heard. Searchlights flashed out below them, and stray beams picked them up. Then the anti-aircraft guns began to bark.

"We're in for a hot time!" cried Jack.

"You said it!" echoed Tom, as he steered the great plane to get into an advantageous position.

Through a glare of light, and amid a hail of shots, the great airships rushed down to hover over the German factories. They would not let go their bombs until in a position to do the most damage, and this took a little time.

"How about it, Tom?" asked Jack, for he was anxious to begin dropping the bombs.

"Just another minute. We'll go down a little lower, and so do all the more damage."

And down the airship went. She was hit several times, for shrapnel was bursting all around, but no material damage was done, though one of the observers was wounded.

"Now!" suddenly signaled Tom.

"There they go!" shouted Jack, and he released bomb after bomb from the retaining devices.

Down they dropped, to explode on striking, and the loud detonations could be heard even above the roar of the motors. Tom noted that the other machine was also doing great destruction, and he saw that their object had been accomplished.

Several fires broke out below them in different parts of the factory property, and soon the Germans had to give so much attention to saving what they could, that their fire against the hostile airships noticeably slackened.

"Any more bombs left, Jack?" asked Tom.

"A few," answered his chum.

"Let 'em have it now. We're right over a big building that seems to be untouched."

Down went the bombs, and such an explosion resulted that it could mean but one thing. They had set off a munition factory. This, as the boys afterward learned, was the case.

So great was the blast that the great plane skidded to one side, and a moment later there came a cry of alarm from some of the crew.

"What's the matter?" shouted Tom.

"Out of control," was the answer. "One of the motors has stopped, and we've got to go down."

"Can't we go up?"

"No!" was the despairing answer. "We've got to land within the German lines."

And down the great Italian plane went, while her sister ship of the air sailed safely off, for it would have been foolhardy for her to have tried to come to the rescue.

The crew worked desperately to send their craft up again, but it was useless. Lower and lower she went, fortunately not being fired at, so great was the confusion caused by the destruction of the factories.

"Take her down as far away as possible from this scene," said Tom to one of his men. "If we land in a lonely place we may be able to make repairs and get up again."

"I will," was the answer.

Through the light from the burning buildings, a spot in a level field was selected for a landing. And down the Italian plane went.

A hasty examination showed little wrong with the motor, and this little was quickly repaired.

But the hope of getting the airship to rise again was frustrated, for just as the raiding party was about to take its place in the machine again, a company of German soldiers came running over the fields, demanding the surrender of the intrepid men of the air. There was nothing else to do—no time to set the craft on fire.

So it fell into the hands of the Germans! Tom, Jack and the others were prisoners!

CHAPTER XXV

THE ESCAPE

"Well, this is tough luck!"

"Tough is no name for it, Jack. It's the worst ever! I don't suppose they'll do a thing to us after what we did to the factories."

"No. We certainly scotched 'em good and proper. Everything went off like a tea party, except our coming down. And we could have gotten up again, only those Germans didn't give us a chance."

"You can't blame 'em for that."

"No, I suppose not. But it's hard lines. I wonder why they're keeping us here?"

Tom and Jack were talking thus while held prisoners by the Germans, after the airship raid over the Rhine. It was an hour after they had been forced to descend.

So sudden had been the rush of the German infantry that no chance was had to destroy the great Italian plane, and it, and all the crew, including the two Air Service boys, had been overpowered, and disarmed. They were thrust into what might pass for a guardhouse, and then, a guard having been posted, the other soldiers hurried back to aid in fighting the fire which had been started in the great factories, and which was rapidly spreading to all the German depot.

"Well, it's worth being captured to think of the damage we've inflicted on the Huns this night," observed Jack, as he stood with Tom in the midst of their fellow prisoners.

"That's right. We don't need to be ashamed of our work, especially as we've helped put the big guns out of business. I reckon the Boches won't treat us any too well, when they know what we've done."

"And the other plane got away, they tell me," observed one of the French crew.

"Yes, I saw her rise and light out for home, after dropping a ton or so of bombs on this district," said Tom. "Well, she can go back and report a success."

"And let the folks know we're prisoners," said Jack. "It's tough luck, but it had to be, I suppose! We're lucky to be alive."

"You said it," agreed Tom. "We came through a fierce fire, and it's a wonder that we weren't all shot to pieces. As it is, the plane is as good as ever."

"Yes, and if we could only get out to it, and start it going we could escape," observed one of the Frenchmen bitterly. "There she is now, on as good a starting field as one could wish!"

From their stockade of barbed wire they could look out and see, by the glare of the flames, that the great plane stood practically undamaged. A good landing had been made, but, unfortunately, in the midst of the German ammunition depot section.

"Whew, that was a fierce one!" exclaimed Jack, as a loud explosion fairly shook the place where they were held prisoners. "Some ammunition went up that time."

Indeed the explosion did seem to be a disastrous one, for there was considerable shouting and the delivering of orders in German following the blast. Many of the soldiers who had been summoned to stand on guard about the barbed-wire stockade, where the captured raiders were held, were summoned away, leaving only a small number on duty.

But as these were well armed, and as the wire stockade was a strong one, and as Jack, Tom and the others had nothing with which to make a fight, they were as safely held as though guarded by a regiment.

"There goes another!" cried Jack, as a second detonation, almost as loud as the first, shook the ground. "Some of our bombs must have been time ones."

"No," said Tom. "What's probably happening is that the fire is reaching stores of ammunition, one after the other. This whole place may go up in a minute."

That seemed to be the fear on the part of the Germans, for more orders were shouted, and all but two of the soldiers guarding the captives were summoned away from the wire stockade.

There had been a bright flare of fire after the second explosion, but this soon died away, and the shouts and commands of the officers directing the fire-fighting force could be heard.

Tom and Jack were standing near the wire barrier trying to look out to see what was going on beyond a group of ruined factory buildings, and at the same time casting longing eyes at the great aeroplane which seemed only waiting for them, when the two boys became aware of a figure which appeared to be slinking along the side of the stockade. This figure acted as though it desired to attract no attention, for it kept as much as possible in the shadows.

"Did you see that?" asked Jack of his churn in a low voice.

"Yes. What do you make it out to be?"

"He isn't a German soldier, for he isn't in uniform. Have any of our crowd found a way out of this place by any chance?"

"I don't know. If they have—"

The boy's words were broken off by a low-voiced call from the slinking figure. It asked:

"Are you American, French or English prisoners?"

"Some of each variety," answered Jack, while at the sound of that voice Tom Raymond felt a thrill of hope.

"If you get out, is there a chance for you to get away in your aircraft?" the figure in the shadow questioned. "Be careful, don't let the guards hear."

"There are only two, and they're over at the front gate," said Jack, as Tom drew nearer in order better to hear the tones of that voice. "They seem more occupied in watching the fire than in looking at us," went on Jack.

"Good!" exclaimed the man. "Now listen. I am an American, and I was captured by the Germans, through spy work, some time ago, in Paris. I was brought here, and they have been trying to force me to disclose the secret of some of my inventions.

"I refused, and was sentenced to be shot to-morrow. But to-night you fortunately raided this place. My prison was one of the places to be blown up, and I managed to escape, without being hurt much. I heard that they had captured the crew of one of the airships, and I came to see if I could help. They don't know yet that I'm free, and I have two hand grenades.

"Now listen carefully. I'll throw the grenades at the front gate. By shattering that it may be possible for you to get out. The two sentries, will have to take the chances of war. If you get out can you get away in your airship?"

"Yes, and we can take you with us—Dad!" exclaimed Tom in a tense whisper.

"Who speaks?" hoarsely asked the man in the shadow of the stockade.

"It is I—your son—Tom Raymond! Oh, thank heaven I have found you at last!" exclaimed Tom, and he tried to stretch his hand through the barbed wire, but it was too close.

"Is it really you, Tom, my boy?" asked Mr. Raymond in a broken voice, full of wonder.

"Yes! And to think I should find you here, of all places!" whispered Tom. "I won't stop now to ask how it happened. Can you throw those grenades at the gate?"

"I can, and will! Tell your friends to run back to the far end of the stockade to avoid being hurt. I can crouch down behind some of the ruined walls."

Tom and Jack quickly communicated the good news to their friends, that a rescue was about to be attempted. It was a desperate chance, but they were in the mood for such.

The two guards alone remaining of the force that had been posted about the stockade were so distracted by the fires and explosions around them, and so fearful of their own safety, that they did not pay much attention to the prisoners. So when Tom and Jack passed the word, and the airship crew ran to the end of the stockade and crouched down to avoid injury when the hand grenades should be exploded, the guards paid little attention.

Mr. Raymond, for it was indeed he, crawled to a position of vantage, and then threw the hand grenades. They were fitted with short-time fuses, and almost as soon as they fell near the stockade gate they exploded with a loud report. A great hole was torn in the ground, and one of the sentries was killed while the other was so badly injured as to be incapable of giving an alarm. The gate was blown to pieces.

"Come on!" cried Tom to his friends, as he saw what his father had done. "It's now or never, before they rush in on us."

They raced to the breach in the wire wall of the stockade. Mr. Raymond, springing up from where he had taken refuge behind a pile of refuse, was there to greet those he had saved, and he and Tom clasped hands silently in the gloom that was lighted up by the fires and the bursts of light from the munition explosions.

"Oh, Dad! And it's really you!" murmured Tom.

"Yes, my boy! I never expected to see you again. Did you know I was here?"

"I never dreamed of it! But don't let's stop to talk. We must get to the airship at once! But you are wounded, Dad!"

"Nothing but a splinter from a bomb. It's only a cut on the head, Son," and Mr. Raymond wiped away the blood that trickled down on his face.

The newly freed prisoners lost no time. With a rush they made for the airship. If they could only get aboard and start it off all would yet be well. Could they do it?

Momentary silence had followed the detonation of the two hand grenades thrown by Mr. Raymond, but now there came yells of rage from the Germans, disclosing that they had become aware of what was going on.

"Lively, everybody!" cried Tom, as he led the way to the big plane.

"Are we all here?" asked Jack.

A rapid count showed that not one of the brave force had been left behind.

"Is there room for me?" asked Mr. Raymond.

"Well, I should say so!"

"If there isn't I'll stay behind," cried Jack.

"No you won't!" exclaimed Tom. "There'll be room all right!"

The running men reached the plane just as they could see, in the light of the burning factories, a squad of Germans rushing to intercept them. In haste they scrambled aboard, and pressed the self-starter on the engine. There was a throbbing roar, answered by a burst of fire from the German rifles, for the place had been so devastated that no machine guns were available just then.

"All aboard?" asked Tom, as he stood ready to put the motors at full speed and send the craft along the ground, and then up into the air.

"All aboard—we're all here!" answered Jack, who had kept count. And Mr. Raymond was included.

Then with a louder roar the motors jumped to greater speed, and the Italian plane started off. In another instant it rose into the air.

With yells of rage the Germans even tried to hold it back with their hands, and, failing, they increased their fire. But though the plane was hit several times, and two on board shot, one later dying from his wounds, the whole party got off. A few minutes later they were above the burning factories, and had a view of the great destruction wrought on the German base. So completely destroyed was it that few defense guns were left in condition to fire at the aeroplane.

"Well, we did that in great shape!" exclaimed Jack, as they were on their way over the Rhine again.

"Couldn't have been better," conceded Tom. "And, best of all, we have dad with us."

"How did it all happen?" asked Jack.

"I don't know. We'll hear the story when we are safe in France."

And safe they were as the gray morning broke. They arrived just as the crew of the other plane were relating, with sorrow, the fall of Tom, Jack and their comrades, and the rejoicing was great when it was known they were safe, and had not only outwitted the Huns, but had brought away a most important prisoner.

"And now let's hear how it all happened," begged Major de Trouville, when the injured had been made as comfortable as possible. There were three of these, and one dead on the plane that returned first.

The story of the attack on the German base was given in detail, and then Mr. Raymond took up the tale from the point where he had landed in Europe.

He had started for Paris, just as he had written Tom, and had taken lodgings in the Rue Lafayette. He went out just before the starting of the bombardment by the big gun, and so escaped injury, but he fell into the hands of some German spies, who were on his trail, and who succeeded, after having drugged him, in getting him into Germany.

The spies had succeeded in getting on the trail of a new invention Mr. Raymond had perfected, and which he had offered to the Allies. He had come to Paris on this business. The Huns demanded that he devote it to their interests, but he refused, and he had been held a prisoner over the Rhine, every sort of pressure being brought to bear on him to make him accede to the wishes of his captors.

"But I refused," he said, "and they decided I should be shot. Whether this was bluff or not I don't know. But they never got a chance at me. In the night I heard, in my prison, the sound of explosions, and I soon realized what had happened. It was your bold airship raid, and one of the bombs burst my prison. I ran out and saw the Italian planes in the air.

"What then happened you know better than I, but what you probably do not know is that you very likely owe your lives to a dispute that arose between the German infantry and the air squadron division," and he indicated Tom, Jack and the others who had been in the stockade.

"How was that?" asked Jack.

"The airmen claimed you as their prey, and the infantrymen said they were entitled to call you theirs. So, even in the midst of the fire and destruction, the commandant had to order you put in the stockade until he could decide whose prisoners you were. The infantrymen said they had captured you, but the airmen said their fire had brought down your plane."

"Well, that was partly true," said Tom. "But it was an explosion from below that knocked us out temporarily. But we're all right now. And so are you, aren't you, Dad?"

"Yes, but I worried a lot, not knowing what had happened to you, Tom, and being unable to guess what would happen to me. I was in the hands of clever and unscrupulous enemies. How clever they were you can judge when I tell you they took me right out of Paris. Perhaps the bombardment made it easier. But tell me—what of the big guns?"

"Some of them are out of commission, thanks to your brave boy and his comrades," said Major de Trouville.

"Good!" cried Mr. Raymond. "Some rumor to that effect sifted in to me there, but it seemed too good to be true. The Germans must be wild with rage."

"I guess they are," admitted Jack.

"And it would have gone hard with you if they had found you were the ones responsible," went on Tom's father. "As soon as I was out of my prison and saw the state of affairs, I managed to get the grenades, and I decided to rescue the airship men if I could. I never dreamed my own son would be among them, or that I might be brought away."

And now it but remains to add that because of their exploits Tom and Jack received new honors at the hands of the grateful French, and, moreover, were promoted.

Mr. Raymond, who had steadfastly refused to reveal the secret of his invention to the Huns, immediately turned it over to the Allies.

Word of Mr. Raymond's safety and of the success of Tom and Jack was sent to those in Bridgeton, and that city had new reasons for being proud of her sons.

But the war was not over, and the Germans might be expected to develop other forms of frightfulness besides the long-range guns, which, for the time being, were silenced. However, the destruction of the factories and ammunition stores by the raid over the Rhine was a blow that told heavily on the Hun.

"Well, it seems there's another vacation coming to us," said Tom to Jack one morning, as they walked away from the breakfast table in their mess.

"Yes? Well, I think we can use it. What do you say to a run into Paris to see your father? He's surely there now, and I'd like to have a talk with him."

"With—him?" asked Tom, and there was a peculiar smile on his face.

"Of course," said Jack.

"Oh," was all Tom answered, but he laughed heartily.

And so, with Tom and Jack on their way to Paris, for a brief respite from the war, we will take leave of them for a time. That they were destined to take a further part in the great struggle need not be doubted, for the Air Service boys were not the ones to quit until the world had been made a decent place in which to live.

THE END